Family Feeling

Family Feeling

a novella & five stories by
Jean Ross Justice

Prairie Lights Books
Iowa City
Distributed by the University of Iowa Press

Prairie Lights Books, Iowa City 52240
Copyright © 2014 by Jean Ross Justice
Printed in the United States of America
Design by Sara T. Sauers

Printed on acid-free paper

LCCN: 2013953656
PAPERBACK ISBNS: 978-0-9859325-4-1, 0-9859325-4-6
E-BOOK ISBNS: 978-0-9859325-6-5, 0-9859325-6-2

Contents

Family Feeling

&

Family Feeling

⳥

· I ·

GARRETT OVERHOLT WAS reading a letter from his former wife, Joy.

> Dear Garrett,
>   I'm sure you'll be surprised to learn that I mean the "dear." You'll be surprised at this communiqué in general, but I want, as they say, to put my affairs in order, incl. my emotional affairs.
>   Maggie has been for a visit and it was a good one, but she needed to get back to our three dear grandchildren. (Is her having a big family a reproach to us, Garrett?) But I see I'm drawing out the suspense without meaning to. I'm seriously sick, Garrett.
>   And I'm asking you to come see me, however briefly. We handled things in a relatively civilized way (except for that one night). But I'd like to leave behind something better than that, something greater than forgiveness—maybe *transcendent* is expecting too much, but our feelings purified.

I

Transcendent; purified. He could see her pondering the words, pleased to find the right ones.

> I'm getting used to my new situation. *Terminal!* An ugly word, suggesting dirty bus stations. I tell myself the future always has an element of the unknown.
>
> I read, though I sometimes have trouble concentrating. The help expects me to watch TV; they like to hear it babbling in the background. I sit and think. I hope to gain at least an insight or two about this condition. I imagine reaching some remarkable conclusion and being—suddenly!—unable to express it.
>
> Anyway, please come. I'm in Cedar Key. It's a quiet place on the Gulf, and maybe that will be an inducement, though of course it's better in the winter. Still, it's a good place.
>
> Love,
>
> Joy

In the lower left corner: "Cedar Key, FL, a day in May, in the year of our Lord 1996."

He was reading the letter for the second time. It was early evening. The hillside backyard beyond the window of the study where he sat was a sea of green treetops; the house blocked some of the late afternoon sunlight from it, but the light showed in the tops of the tallest trees. Down the hall his wife was singing to their baby son.

"Go-olden slumbers kiss your eyes . . ." She had a lovely voice and lovely long legs. He believed she liked him to hear the evening lullaby. Her keen awareness of him was usually pleasing.

Both times he'd read the letter he'd thought, Oh, Joy, I'm so

2

sorry, I'm truly sorry, so very sorry. He was eager to tell her that. But as for going to see her—impossible. He hadn't quite found the reason, he couldn't quite put his finger on it but it was out there somewhere and would come to him.

> And I will
> Sing a
> Lull-uh-by.
> Luh-ull-a-by.

Except for that one night, Joy said, they'd been civilized about it. Yes, that night had been uncivilized. Her rage had stunned him.

"How can you bear to be so typical, so typically late-middle-aged faithless and philandering? Oh, men, men, men. The power of new sex. 'Cal-Cal-Caliban, get a new mistress, be a new man.'" At the moment he couldn't think where that came from. They knew the same things, and he'd introduced her to some of them. "I hope she falls for someone else and leaves you for him in ten or fifteen years, when you'll be needing somebody to look after you, maybe. Oh, I hope you'll need somebody to look after you, I hope you fall apart. God, how I hate you. I better get out of here before I start throwing things." How steely, how mean spirited, this dreamy woman he thought he knew had become.

"Joy, Joy, this isn't like you—"

"How do you know what's like me? If you knew me you'd love me too much to do this. Goodbye, Garrett, goodbye, good riddance."

When he went into the kitchen the next morning she wasn't up, though she had regular habits, one of them to rise around 7:30. It felt very quiet in the house. It was Sunday, a sunny Sunday that might have been a nice day.

They allowed themselves bacon on Sundays, and he cooked and ate his alone, the Sunday papers strewn over the table.

He'd read the papers and waited. An hour passed. Still hearing no sounds from upstairs, he went up and listened outside the door of the bedroom she'd occupied alone last night, he having moved to the guest room. No sounds from inside, and he knocked on the door. "Hello! Are you up?" meaning, Are you all right? Amid the tangle of his thoughts there was the awareness that if she'd taken something, nobody else knew what he'd told her last night. Had he really thought that? And had thoughts of an overdose (of what he had no idea) been pure ego? But in this time of upheaval, who knew . . .

She'd called from inside the room, something he couldn't make out. Soon she opened the door and said, neutrally, "You woke me."

Down in the kitchen she said, "Bacon morning!" and almost nothing else.

He couldn't keep from talking; there was so much he wanted to insist on. "Listen, didn't you enjoy some of our years, wasn't it worth something, can't you look back on it with some pleasure?"

She cut him off. "Save your breath."

After breakfast she said, "I trust you're packing?" and he got to it.

After he'd loaded the car he came to find her and said, "I'm sorry. I'd recommend you as a wife to anyone! Maybe I can become a Mormon, some renegade sect, and have two—"

"Indeed. You're ready to go? Wonderful." She gave him a vague smile and turned away.

When, later, they met on business (he was surprised and a little disappointed that she didn't want the house), she scarcely looked at him. She gave him a faint, neutral smile, as if he were someone she'd met once at a party and barely remembered.

That had been almost four years ago. And now the letter.

His wife, Sophie, was coming down the hall; she stuck her head in the door. "Golden slumbers kissed his eyes," she sang softly.

"Come on in." She slid gracefully onto his lap, her arm around his neck. "I have this letter from Joy. She's sick, she wants me to come see her. Clear up any unpleasantness lingering from the past. She thinks she's done for. I hope not, but that's what she says." He decided not to hand her the letter. "I'm sorry as I can be—but what a trip. What a trip." Sophie would help him find the reason not to go that hovered just beyond his reach.

Sophie kissed him. There was a vague alien smell about her, partly a nursery smell, he thought, but her warm weight on his lap was sweet, and he smoothed her knee through her skirt.

"Oh God. That's terrible. I'm so sorry. And you have to go, don't you."

· 2 ·

HENRY

If I mull over it long enough, I may figure out why I've come home: I may figure out which of the various reasons that occur to me is the true one.

My father thinks I've come to check on him. He knows he's declining; he often wonders, nervously, if there's some important thing he's forgotten, something he was supposed to do this very day, this very minute.

Mornings when I go into the kitchen and find him eating breakfast, he may have forgotten that I'm here; he looks mildly surprised. Is he pleased? Can't tell. "The cereal's up there, help yourself."

"I'm going to be with you a while," I told him. "I'll be here to take you to your doctor's appointments and grocery shopping and all that."

"Oh, Dwight always takes me. He doesn't mind." Dwight lives next door. Dwight is glad to see me; he's greeted me warmly.

My father's face, basically sallow with a little reddish weathering, seems curiously shiny, as if it's been washed with soap and not rinsed. His hair is sparse, more gray than white, and sternly parted on the side, a bit low. He's slim as ever. But his health has been iffy in the last few years.

In fact, my cousin Pris called a few months ago and suggested it might be time to talk him into going to assisted living. I told her he sounded okay. But when I decided I had to drive away to somewhere else, I thought, this is a reason for going home.

But mostly I'm here because this is where, when you go there, they have to take you in. I say this to Dad the second or third morning, giving Frost credit; he looks a little puzzled. "Well, sure. Of course." I'm here because I believe in cutting my losses. With a failing business, you don't need to wait for it to fail completely. A failing marriage? My marriage feels somehow suspended. Anyway, it gave me pleasure to zoom off up the interstate and drive, drive, drive away. I can imagine better destinations, but this one will do, and here I am. Home.

Home is this respectable, respected big squarish white house, in this North Carolina town where many of the houses come from the same era, the early 1900s. The house has a front porch on two sides and a little second floor balcony. It's big enough that, if neither my brother Garrett nor I choose to live in it when

we inherit it, its future might be to house some business enterprise—a bed-and-breakfast, a funeral home.

My father makes a change—I won't say improvement—in it
every so often. There's a deck tacked onto the back now, looking a
little raw and out of place, being nearly a hundred years younger
than the house, and he's added several skylights. Walking toward
it, you can see a couple of the little bubbles on the roof of this
time-honored house, and it looks a little odd. But he likes these
new things.

Here at home, I have a project in mind, though I can't pretend it's why I've come: family history; genealogy. Going to old
cemeteries, looking for old-home places. It's a late-middle-age
pursuit; now, at fifty-four, I may be ripe for it. Looking for old
family graveyards and abandoned homesteads will at least get
me out of the house.

It was a week after I came, when I was just settling in, that the
old orange Volkswagen bus came putt-putting down the street
one afternoon.

It was packed to the gills, stuff stacked up to the windows, a
sort of attic on wheels. Somebody fleeing an old hippie enclave?
I saw it from the window over my desk upstairs and was startled
when it pulled up in front of the house. A young woman emerged
and extricated a small child from a car seat lost somewhere among
the boxes and bags. She took the child, a toddler, by the hand and
began to walk it slowly up the walk, then picked it up and headed
for the front door. For some reason it made me think of some old
cartoon—a woman carrying a baby to a door to demand help,
accusing someone of fatherhood (what have you been up to,
Dad?). I was mesmerized for a moment, then leaped up.

It was Sophie, my sister-in-law, someone I scarcely knew. She'd been my brother Garrett's wife only a few years and I hadn't seen much of them. I hustled down the stairs.

"Hey—! He didn't tell me you were coming!"

She was as surprised as I'd been. "Oh, he didn't know I was coming. *I* didn't know I was coming. And I didn't know you were here."

It came to us that we should kiss; we did. The child, hanging behind her, didn't approve and let out a little squawk.

"Sam, this is Uncle Henry. Say hello." I said hello. Sam, plumpish and dark haired, was mum. "Garrett's gone, and I wanted to get out of that house. I thought—your dad here alone, he could use some company, some help. I think I need some kind of help, I'm not sure what, till I get on my feet. Get my bearings."

What would it take to get her on her feet? They were long, slender feet in flip-flops. She was tall and slim, with long dark hair done up raggedly in a ponytail. The few times I'd been around her, she hadn't projected her personality very forcefully, one might say; she was the new person in the family, and may have been getting her bearings, seeing how the land lay. My wife works hard at keeping an open mind, but she may have felt some semi-secret disapproval of the much younger second wife who appeared to have played a part in my brother's divorce. It wasn't something I'd given much thought to. Garrett and Sophie were up in Virginia and I lived in Florida. Now here we were, back home at a point in between.

"Of course," I said, "there's plenty of room." It seemed possible my father wouldn't place her instantly either.

If he didn't, though, he didn't let on; he's become cagy about what he's forgotten. Anyway, when eventually he came into the kitchen where we sat having Coca-Colas, I said quickly, "Sophie's come to see us—she and Garrett are taking a little vacation from each other," and he laughed cheerfully. Sophie was on her feet, leaving Sam balanced somewhat perilously on a straight chair; she was hugging my father. "Is it okay, Dad?" (Had she always called him Dad?)

"Oh, certainly, certainly." At length, in his measured way, "Everybody needs a little vacation once in a while." He smiled happily, staring at her as if he'd never seen her before. He'd never seen her without Garrett, of course, and that had changed the picture, like a chemical combination with one element removed.

We were waiting for her to tell us more. Specifically, more about her and Garrett. She talked about the trip down, her fears for the old vehicle, the details of its history, and the shape her mother was in. She couldn't go to her mother's because her mother had lately moved into a retirement place where children were not allowed. "Thoughtless of her!" She tried to laugh. "They let kids visit but for a limited time, not move in." I thought: A limited time may be all you'll need. "She's remarried. I don't know this new husband at all well."

We went on waiting, through getting the ancient baby bed down from the attic, unloading the van, getting sheets on the bed in one of the bedrooms, and then, through dinner, sitting at the round oak table in the kitchen. My father has an arrangement with a place called Margie's Kitchen to bring him prepared meals for the freezer. These are in single meal-sized portions, so we mostly ate different things. She took an eggplant parmesan and fixed an egg for Sam. "We'll go grocery shopping tomorrow," I said, playing the conscientious host. I wondered how long she'd be here. Funny that we were here at the same time; it felt a little awkward.

It may seem strange that we didn't ask her any questions but we didn't know her well, and we may have feared some outrush of emotion. She'd tell us in her own good time.

The child stayed up later than any of us had hoped. My father and I sat in the living room, waiting for her to come back downstairs; there was the soft, distant drone of her voice upstairs reading to him, reading and reading. Dad murmured, "How long do you think . . . ?"

"Your guess is as good as mine."

Then she was back downstairs, with an apologetic smile. "He was kind of wound up." She sat down with us for a minute, then said, "Do you mind if I play the piano?"

"Oh. No, no. Go ahead. Won't it wake him up?"

"No, once he gets to sleep he's out." She rustled among the music in the piano bench.

She played well enough to do. A few wrong notes and hesitations, when she might jerk her shoulders or make a little sound. This was my mother's music—she'd been a piano teacher—and it was familiar stuff, Schubert's "Serenade" and Mozart's "Rondo alla Turca," and some slightly melancholy Chopin.

My father and I sat listening. The music took the place of explanations. As if it was what we needed to hear at the moment.

At a pause in the playing, Dad said, "Well, I'm about ready to turn in. But you go ahead and play. It won't bother me. I read a while first anyway."

But she gave the piano a little farewell ripple, the way Garrett used to, and murmured, "Oh no. Thanks. I'm pretty tired too."

"I expect so."

I thought: he'll dream about her tonight—dream he's a young man, married, with a young child.

When I turned out my light that night I looked out the window and saw the light from Sophie's room still on, ghostly on the trees and grass below. It was quiet in the house; she must be reading, and I wondered what. Probably she was having trouble sleeping. I pondered the piano-playing. A little self-dramatization? Well, she was young and seemed to be troubled. Garrett gone! I was going to ask her some questions if she didn't spill the beans tomorrow.

With all she had on her mind, it wasn't surprising that she hadn't asked how long I was going to be here.

The next morning she and Sam were in the kitchen when I went down. After we'd dodged around each other and got settled with our cereal and yogurt, I said, "Did you say Garrett left?"

"Yes. He left two weeks ago."

I waited a little while. "Do you know where he is?"

"Yes. He's at Joy's. She's down in Florida." Now she waited a while. "She's sick."

"Oh. That's too bad."

Slowly, slowly, after a wait. "He's gone to look after her."

How wonderful, I opened my mouth to say—one of the nicest things I've known him to do! (That was a joke.) "Well, that seems like a kind thing to do. What's her trouble, I wonder?"

She gave me a bland look and wiped Sam's chin. "They're not married any more, you know." She was different today; yesterday she'd been exhausted from packing and driving and had seemed vulnerable, even weak; today she was more herself, her poise returned, her will firmed up. "She wanted him to come, and he should have visited her, okay! I *urged* him to. It's not like she doesn't have help. Her aunt left her some money. She can afford skilled care, the kind she needs—she has cancer. Go see her, of course, but he didn't have to move in to look after her, which is what he's done. Who knows how long she'll live—maybe six months, a year, who knows? I *hope* she keeps on living. But is he going to stay for the duration?" She was getting up a head of steam.

"Oh, he's staying a while. I see ... Yes, I guess it's a little strange."

"I have a small child—*we* have a small child—"

"Yes."

We fell silent. After a while I asked, "Does he know you're here?"

"Not unless he has extrasensory perception. Which he is far from having. He has very little sense of other people's feelings."

I shook my head sympathetically and poured myself a cup of coffee. Soon she wiped off the old stroller and put Sam in it for a walk. She set off with a kind of grim energy.

She was absorbed in Garrett. Her coming here had something to do with him, of course. Going to report him to his father? It didn't make too much sense. I'd have to tell Garrett she was here; she must know that.

I tried to imagine Garrett and Joy in Cedar Key. I hadn't seen Joy in at least five years. A smart woman, and, at first, when you played Boggle or Scrabble with her, she wanted to make sure you knew it. That was a long time ago when we were just getting acquainted, visiting here at the same time. My mother seemed to have some little unacknowledged reservation about her, at least back then—but my mother wanted her sons' wives to be simply mad about them; she liked the way my wife, Alice, touched my shoulder and patted my arm (however meaningless it might be), the way she gave me a big smile when I came into the room. Joy probably wasn't a big-smile kind of person. Nice, though rather reserved. A kind of ordinary prettiness, gold highlights in her brown hair. She was like Garrett in a lot of ways, inclined to tell you all about what she was reading, sometimes at too much length.

Alice tried to keep in touch with her after the divorce, perhaps out of some notion of duty. But Joy gradually let the communications lapse, as if it was time to leave all of Garrett's family behind.

·3·

Henry got the talent, Garrett got the charm.

Luther Overholt awakened to that thought. It was something the boys' mother once said. True, probably. Henry had the musical talent, the one that had mattered to his mother. Her hopes had been on Henry; Garrett was freer to do what he wanted.

Oh, yes, this morning Henry was in the house. And someone else, who'd come yesterday. The daughter-in-law. Not Henry's wife but Garrett's wife. Sophie.

A little awkward, too. Lonely as Luther had been during the winter, he couldn't help regretting the trouble this was. Before he went to the kitchen for breakfast, he had to consider whether or not his bathrobe was spotty and make sure he'd combed his hair and didn't have bad breath.

And why had they come? What did they want?

"What does she want, you think?" he murmured to Henry that morning. She'd already had breakfast, and she and the child were out on a walk, Henry had said. They sat in the big, bright kitchen with the old noisy white metal cabinets all around, and the white curtains with delicate flower-embroidered borders that his wife, Ruth, had hung at the short windows years ago.

"She wanted to get away from home, she said. Garrett left, to go see Joy—she's sick. Maybe terminally sick. He went to see her, which was good, don't you think, but he's still there, staying on, and Sophie's upset about it."

Luther's thoughts went ranging about the past. "I hated it that he and Joy couldn't iron out their differences, you know. After so many years together. She was a nice girl." Henry gave him a funny look, as though he were forgetting something. (As usual?) Another woman, that was part of it. Oh yes. Another woman: Sophie.

"She didn't know I was here. She had some idea of keeping you company, helping you, something like that."

"Oh. Well. That's very nice."

And what do *you* want? he wanted to ask Henry. To assess my competency, perhaps. His cousin Pris, who paid her inspects every so often, might have tipped Henry off. ("Better check on him, hon. It might be time for assisted living.") At his age, you became self-conscious: they were noticing. They were taking stock, seeing how well you walked, whether you seemed forgetful or stumbled over words.

Then he told himself not to get paranoid. Henry was a little low, and that was a good time to come home, even if home wasn't all it used to be.

Two academic sons, and he was proud of them. Henry hadn't been willing to work for those advanced degrees you needed, though. Maybe Garrett wouldn't have either, but he'd lucked out with his novels; one had won a prize early, and that seemed to let him get by without the further degrees. Two good-looking fellows, taller than he was even before he started losing height. Henry had bulked up, his face fuller, some white sprinkled through his short dark hair and his thick dark brows. Somewhat diffident, given to half-shrugs. Garrett had a thinner face and a quicker, narrow-eyed smile.

With Henry and his mother there'd been the bond of music. At ten or eleven Garrett had decided he wasn't going to study piano any longer, and she let him go. Later, when he had a musical girlfriend, he'd come back to it and studied another year or two. He could play rather well, if not as well as Henry; he liked doing things in a casual, off-hand kind of way and, if he couldn't do them that way, might not do them at all.

Luther and Ruth had wanted their sons to be *polished,* well-brought-up boys. He'd thought to teach them to carve, in their teens; he gathered carving a roast was something fathers knew how to do in good families in town. Out in the country his mother had done the carving, if you could call it that, in the kitchen, but he studied directions in cookbooks, mastered it fairly well, and meant to teach the boys. Henry—plumpish, conscientious, early-teens Henry—watched and seemed to take it in; Garrett smiled his little tight-lidded smile, said, "My wife will know how," and soon slipped away to do something else.

How close the two of them were now he couldn't tell. No bad-mouthing, at least. Politeness wasn't as good as love, but it was something.

How faraway their childhoods seemed, *The Three Billy Goats Gruff* and all those Little Golden Books. Were they really the same people?

Now Henry was here, his music school closed. His wife not along—and he'd gone to a little too much trouble explaining why he hadn't gone with her and her sister on a cruise with old college friends. He sensed that Henry was feeling sorry for himself. Buck up, he wanted to tell Henry: you're still young, still in your fifties.

"Everything goes to you and Garrett, of course. Who else," he'd already said to Henry. "John Bogan has the will. He's still my lawyer." This sort of thing needed to be repeated. There was the house, and a farm a few miles out from town, 95 acres of average land with an average return; once it had had a tenant farmer, now it was rented to the nearest big farmer. A couple of store buildings in town, occupied presently by a beauty shop and a new antiques place. Money in Savings and Loan and some mutual funds and the bank.

And here was Garrett's wife. Would she and Garrett divorce? He was pleased with himself for boldly accepting this unpleasant possibility, so much more common now—and Garrett had divorced once already. Then she'd be out of the picture. Except that there was the grandson. His only grandson, so much younger than the two granddaughters, Henry's and Garrett's one-each. He might think about the grandson later, when things cleared up a little.

After breakfast, Henry put on a cap, which seemed not quite his style, put a small notebook in his shirt pocket, and set out on one of his new genealogical expeditions, looking for abandoned cemeteries and the sites of old home places. Making his way through briers and other people's pastures, asking permission, not always getting it. What difference did it make, seeing where it *was*? It was gone, so very gone.

He folded up the newspaper and sat on, thinking of Garrett's wife. Sophie. Once in a while when he reached for the name he might find instead Joy, the name of the first wife, a member of the family, then gone, which was too bad. Now this wife had to be accepted. *Sophie.*

How would it have been if Henry hadn't been here? The two

of them, Sophie and himself, sitting at meals; would it have been an awkward intimacy, or easier? He decided he liked her. In her time of trouble, she'd chosen to come here, to him.

·4·

Garrett came into Cedar Key in early-evening fog, after a drive on empty roads through desolate, thickly wooded country broken by an occasional run-down little settlement. "Turpentine country," he murmured to himself, without knowing quite what he meant, taking in the pines close to the road. On the other side, a ditch, an open field, then more woods.

Here was the town, little inlets nosing up to the highway that was the main street; it wound along past bait shops, gas stations, and a few unambitious motels. Then a small business district, a grocery, post office, a couple of small but more serious motels. He parked in the convenience store lot and studied Joy's map.

Her rental was a tiny white frame house on a narrow street by the water, the next-door houses small and close, and the ones across the street fifteen feet away.

A blonde woman answered his knock. "Oh, hello, I'm looking—my God, it's you!" Joy in a blonde wig, sick and sallow, but smiling.

"It's me. Come in." The most minute pause before they embraced.

A house of small rooms, furnished in rattan upholstered with bamboo-patterned greenery. "What a great spot! You couldn't get much closer to the water."

"It may not be stylish but it's quiet—one of my favorite places. I intend to have some of what I like—I'm so lucky I can. And so lucky you've come! I bet you want a drink, but we'd better go on out to eat before every place closes up."

"How about some ice water?" He stood against the counter in the small kitchen while she broke out the ice. The back windows gave onto the water. "This is great." She was silent, watching him drink, and he said, "Let's not stand on ceremony. We haven't got that much time. Tell me all about it, anything. Everything?"

"We have some time. I'm not going to die tonight!"

"I mean, a weekend is kind of a short time. So tell me about the treatments—unless you don't like to talk about it."

"Oh, I don't mind," she said as they walked out to the car. "Not much to tell; chemo makes you sick, of course, and they give you pills for the sickness. It's just one pill after another. And pretty soon you don't want to pick up a comb and get a comb full of hair. How do you like me as a blonde?"

"Interesting. Somebody in my department used to say she had more fun when she was a blonde." Maybe that was tactless, considering what fun would be ahead for her.

"Oh, I mean to have fun. Of some sort. It's fun looking out at the water. I took a boat ride to an island across the way that used to flourish in the nineteenth century. That was fun."

Twilight was coming on. In the restaurant street by the water, lights were on everywhere, and people thronged the narrow sidewalks, occasionally stepping out into the street to avoid the congestion.

"Most of the restaurants aren't much good. Keep going, take a right. Go on to the end down there."

It was a restaurant with white tablecloths and candles, half full; there was still a window table. The water was close, out in the half-light. "What are you working on? Tell me a good plot, a good story. Oh, how's Henry? How's your father?"

"They're okay. Henry closed the music school.It wasn't doing well. Things sounded kind of unsettled, last I talked to him. Maybe domestic problems—that's just a feeling I had."

"I guess it runs in the family. Scratch that, it doesn't sound nice. And I intend to end *nice*."

"Oh, we won't think about endings."

"We'll think about them whether we like it or not. Oh, Garrett, it's good to see you. Good of you to come. Did she mind much?"

"Not at all. She thought I should." Was there a flicker of disappointment in her face? He thought of saying, I would have anyway, but he might have to tell some soothing little lies before it was all over; no need to get into what might or might not be true. (Wasn't it possible he'd have seen his duty and come even if Sophie hadn't liked the idea?)

Back at the house, they opened a bottle of wine and sat on the porch in the dark and listened to the water lapping at the shore. "Right after you left, I'd feel really mad off and on. I'd find myself saying 'You silly bastard!' right out loud! It was bad. I guess I shouldn't tell you that. Then I got over it. Particularly after I got sick, all the petty little things seemed so—petty."

"Sure." His thoughts jumped between warm and cool. To have the friendship back, the animosity gone . . . But there were these little provocations, the old anger popping out; it was slightly alarming. She was sick, sick, sick. She hadn't eaten much of the good grouper at dinner. Her eyes seemed larger, large and tired— so much older. Sitting in the restaurant, under the bright lights, he'd had a moment of cold-sweat fear—had he started something he might not be able to handle, something with this woman who, with her blonde fall of hair and sick eyes, could at moments seem a stranger? Here in the dark, on the porch, he felt more at ease.

There was a moon, hidden under a cloud; you could see its spot of light far out on the water.

She pulled her chair closer and reached for his hand. "Oh, I've been lucky. Lucky that Aunt Bet left me some money—she didn't have anyone else to leave it to, poor dear. I never paid her enough attention, it's a sorrow to me. I'm lucky I have a nice daughter and three healthy grandchildren who may remember me a little. Even if I won't see them grow up all the way. I'm lucky I had a good job, and I did well by it. And I did all right as a mother—anyway, I've got a good daughter, that proves something. I've had good books and music . . . Oh, I've been lucky. And I'm lucky you're here with me."

"Good." He took her cool hand and kissed it.

He woke the next morning from a long, peaceful sleep: Sam hadn't come and climbed into bed with them—but a strange room, strange wooden louvers at the windows, motel-ish pictures on the wall—Joy's; Cedar Key.

It was late, past nine. The house was quiet. He opened the door to Joy's room very quietly; she lay in bed, facing the other way, under a sheet, very still. So still, so still . . . He told himself to stay away from morbid fears.

He opened the back door to dazzling sun on quiet water; doves on a neighboring wire fluttered up with delicate screechings. A block away at the convenience store he found a copy of the Gainesville paper and lucked out with a copy of the *New York Times* of the day before, as she'd said he might.

In the tiny kitchen he found some granola and ate a bowl of it. He was relieved to hear sounds from her room, then her feet padding along to the bathroom. She appeared, a dark-printed scarf tied neatly around her head. "How lovely to find you here."

"Want me to do some eggs? I saw some in the fridge." He was getting her a bowl and handing out the granola.

"Only if you want some. Oh, it's bright and lovely. You could walk around town before it gets too hot. The pelicans on the dock are great. But you're going to be bored, no way around it."

"Bored in a new place? I won't be."

Maggie called after breakfast, while Joy was slowly getting dressed. "Dad! You're there. That's wonderful, I didn't know— how good of you." This was warmer than the last time they'd talked. She'd been slow to forgive him for the divorce. It had disappointed him—such predictable, ungenerous behavior. "I didn't like the idea of her going down there by herself but you know her, she can be stubborn. I tried to talk her out of it or at least get her to take somebody with her. How long can you stay?"

"Just the weekend, that's the plan."

"Well, if there're any likely looking neighbors you could talk to—I don't guess that's a good idea, though. She's so independent. I do know some people in Gainesville and I looked up their number for her, the Aders. They're nice, and I'm getting in touch with them. Have her call them if she needs help, okay? Here's the number . . . You're nice to do this. Maybe you could stay a little longer?"

Joy walked with him to the dock. A few fishermen, some in chairs; pelicans walked among them. "They look as though their noses are running. Don't they look wise, though. Possessors of some age-old wisdom."

"Who said that?"

"Me."

"Want to have lunch down here?"

"I'm kind of tired already. I'd rather go back and maybe have some soup."

That night, after dinner, they again sat on the porch. The water was still and almost colorless, only a faint shell pink tone from the sky. A small plane buzzed in the sky, then was gone.

"There's an airstrip. Probably some drugs get unloaded out there, I wouldn't know. There was an accident not so long ago. These two couples flew over from Gainesville or maybe it was Jacksonville in a private plane, for dinner, and they were flying back when they got confused—the sea and the sky sort of merge around dusk, they say, if you're not used to it, flying. Anyway, they went down in the drink. Terrible. I know they weren't ready to go, but it seems like a kind of beautiful way to perish, heading into sea and sky . . . "

"Really?" He saw them screaming, holding onto the plane, perhaps for agonized hours. He opened his mouth to say, There is no beautiful way to perish, but caught himself.

She was quiet for a while. "I read this book about dying—Elisabeth Kübler-Ross. I've read a lot about dying. Thought a lot about dying. I'm becoming kind of an expert on dying."

Stop it, stop it. "So will we all, eventually. I'd stop thinking about it if I were you. You're not going to die tonight." She'd said it yesterday; he'd say it today. "You have any good reading? There's a library, isn't there? You didn't bring a Boggle set, by any chance? Cards?"

"Those card games we played are kind of boring. You know,

22

when you have only so much time left you want to do things that are *meaningful*. And what are they? What can I do that's meaningful?" She seemed to wait for him to answer. "Visit here with you! Actually I'm keeping a journal, sort of for the grandchildren, when they're old enough. I'll send it to you. You can pass it on to Maggie. Or maybe I'll be giving it to her—however it works out . . . Promise me not to use it, though—it's not to be used in fiction. Okay?"

"Of course. That's a funny idea, that I'd try to use it."

"I thought you'd never been one to let anything go to waste. Well—listen, I thought of a plot for you. Someone who's terminally ill and tired of waiting for the moment to come decides to go to Holland, where they allow assisted suicide. But something happens to him—maybe he meets someone?—and he starts enjoying life so that he changes his mind and wants to keep on living. Maybe he even begins to recover. Or maybe he wasn't terminally ill, just something chronic, and terribly depressed, enough to kill himself. What do you think? I'll give you the plot, gratis."

"It has possibilities, I'll say that."

After a silence she said, "I think about the exact moment, you know. Of course they fill you with morphine, which is probably a good thing. Listening to nice music, holding the hand of somebody I love. I guess this sounds soupy. Say 'love' and you're at risk of sounding soupy. But you have to risk it, at the end."

"Of course." On the horizon, far away over the water, there was sudden lightning, a jagged vertical streak. "Let's go inside. I picked up some movies at the rental place—you can decide what we want to watch."

He packed the next night, ready to drive away in the morning.

23

Had they covered the important things, had they reached a peace? He wasn't sure. The split, the re-marriage—why get into that? Still, it hung between them.

It felt like the middle of the night when his door opened. Joy came over to his bed and stood there in the dark. In the light from the open door he could make out her pale face, her bald head. "Come sleep in my room, please. I'm kind of panicky. Will you? There's a cot in my closet—they like to rent this place to a houseful when they can."

He followed her to her room, set up the cot beside her bed, dodging the sight of her baldness, and went back to his room for sheet and pillow. Settled on the cot, he reached for her ready hand and held it firmly.

In a few minutes she murmured, "Heat my Bed Buddy for me?" and handed him what felt like a stuffed stocking. "In the microwave. My feet are freezing. High for a minute then turn it and do it another minute."

He came back with it and slipped it into her bed, fumbling for her feet. "Ah, wonderful. Thank you."

He lay awake. Probably he'd be awake now half the night. He'd thought she was asleep when she whispered, as if someone nearby mustn't hear them, "Don't go tomorrow."

"All right."

"Well. Sure. A few more days?" There was disappointment in Sophie's voice. "Hadn't she been down there by herself before you went?" He called her every day, pacing along outside just beyond the back porch. The connection was always poor here.

"Yes . . . But she had a kind of panic attack last night. I need to stick around just a little longer. I miss you, darling."

"Um-m, kiss kiss, you don't know how much I miss you. Let Sam say hello."

Sam breathed into the phone and murmured slowly, "Daddy, Daddy," then after a long pause said slowly, "Bye-bye."

·5·

HENRY

The hills that cluster around the river here are high; a little range of them runs on into the next county. The tallest is called Cheeke Mountain after one of the families who lived up there back in the 1800s, but it's flattering it to call it a mountain; it's a kind of elevated plateau. There was an early settlement up there; why it passed I don't know, but some sources say it was after a typhoid epidemic. It's gone back to nature and is now a state park.

Some of the family lived up there. If my father knows where exactly, he doesn't say; he's indifferent to my researches. I thought there might be a family cemetery. I meant to tramp around up there just to be doing it. As if I would learn something just by walking where the old folks had walked.

So I made my way up an old woods road and turned off into the thick woods; tramping along, noisy among the still trees and thick undergrowth.

After half an hour, some encouragement: traces of a foundation, a modest rectangle of stones in the ground, a little tumble of collapsed stones on one side. Could have been a house or an outbuilding, a smokehouse, say; not big enough for a barn. There might be a family burying ground somewhere around.

Maybe it was my lucky day. Not yet, though. No pieces of thin slate rock sticking up from the ground, half-buried, names and dates scratched on them. Nothing else at all.

Onward. And after another mile or two—it was getting hotter and buggier—a rose bush. A rose bush.

It was a poor scraggly thing of two pink blooms, crooked, almost crowded out by wild growth pushing against it, but it said homestead, and I began to quarter the ground around it.

I wanted it to be the rose of a certain ancestor, our great-great-great grandfather. He was an unlucky Tory. It's that man's grave I'd most like to find. I want to see whether he made it back to this country after he had to flee. I'd read about him in a family history a distant cousin had written up.

He was a man who had some minor office and chose to keep his promise to the King of England. He had sworn an oath, and he didn't mean to join the rebellion. Naturally he had to flee. Oh, they were vicious, those patriots. He had to live in the swamps, hiding out, stealing food by night; perhaps his family sneaked some to him—I would like to think so—or maybe the patriots were watching his family. He made his way to Canada, barely escaping with his life. His property was confiscated, of course.

There were two sons, still adolescent or early teens when he left. When they were grown, they took an oath of loyalty to the new country, or whatever you did at the time to prove yourself a patriot. They petitioned to have the property back, and the home place, where their mother had been permitted to live, was given back, along with some of the other land they'd lost.

And I think of them with regret, even a little anger. Did they never think of journeying to Canada to find their father? Some of the American Tories lived in England for perhaps a decade (I haven't researched this), then returned to the U.S. And their mother—didn't she want to join her husband? What kind of love was that? She may have been a little old for the journey, of course, and maybe without a lot of ready money. But there's something too matter-of-fact about the way that family adapted. I wish they'd thought more about the virtue of keeping your promises, as their father had done, and about family feeling. I wish they'd suffered alongside their father in the swamps, living off the land; I'd respect them more. Keeping your promises, honoring your vows. Loyalty. Family feeling!

I don't know why this man's life has gripped me.

Am I feeling sorry for myself?

I was wondering if he came back after things had died down, after ten years or so. They might have kept it quiet; anyway, the people who piece those family histories together are at the mercy of a few faulty memories, a few old family tales, a few headstones in abandoned cemeteries, dates scratched on slate rock thin as a plate. It would have pleased me to turn up a headstone for him.

Nothing turned up anywhere near the rose bush. It wouldn't have been as old as the Revolution anyway. I gave up and went home. Time for the midday meal.

My father was eating a dish of cottage cheese at the kitchen table. I made some tuna salad for us and for Sophie, though there was no sign of her at the moment.

I had a funny thought, and I said to my father, "At least one person in town is going to assume Sophie is my wife—my second wife, don't you suppose?"

"Very likely," my father said, without really thinking about it.

I taught at the university for some years but I was always a kind of adjunct even when it wasn't called that. I didn't have advanced degrees. I could get argumentative about this. MAs and PhDs don't guarantee the best teaching. I had a year of graduate school in English, after doing mostly music in college, but didn't stick around long enough to get a master's; a job turned up and I took it. Later I left the university for a community college where I had more autonomy and respect, but the students were somewhat disappointing; I suppose I was jaded. I gave up that job and started a music school, teaching piano. I am not a virtuoso player, but I'm good; you don't have to be concert grade to teach well. I hired a couple of good teachers, and we flourished for a time, but then our rent was raised, my best teacher left for New York, and I had trouble replacing her.

It was a foolish idea to start with. I'd been dreaming, thinking it would be good to have my own enterprise, dealing with something I loved. Probably I imagined it a way it wouldn't be. I overheard a teacher saying, "This is a *nocturne*. Nocturne means it's at night. Think of night on a beautiful lake—" Ideas like that didn't occur to me—though of course you want to help the pupil get the feeling of the piece. I was learning as I went along.

One man, grown but a beginner, asked me to name the most difficult piano piece there was. I said maybe one of the Mephisto Waltzes. That's what he wanted to learn. I told him we'd better start on something easier. He gave up after a month or so.

There were six or seven pretty good years before it became a losing proposition. So much for pursuing my artistic inclinations. No point in trying to figure it all out now. Time to cut my losses.

Alice, my wife, raised her brows and was uncharacteristically silent at the bad news. She didn't strike me as totally sympathetic, shall we say. She hadn't wanted me to start the school in the first place. Do I expect too much? This was a bad time in my life, and

I needed some support, some reassurance. Freely given, without begging for it.

Alice has an orderly mind and a businesslike approach to life.

I always had contempt (though that may put it too strongly) for men who fell for beauty queens; I wanted a serious person, a competent person. A musical person, too. Alice and I were both taking piano in college; she also played the flute. I like the flute—a nice instrument. It's a while now since she's played it.

Marriage is a speculative venture. When you're young and the juices are flowing and you're attracted to someone, all the person's qualities are fresh and remarkable; you accept them without question. Only later, as they harden into habits, they may begin to seem commonplace. You don't know a person till you've lived with them for some time. It's probably good that more people live together before marriage now.

Alice doesn't read the kind of avant-garde stuff Garrett and Joy kept up with, and she doesn't worry about whether everything she says sounds smart and original; she's willing to say what might be called the commonplace but pleasant thing. I suspect Joy would have died rather than tell someone to have a nice day. Not Alice.

She has a natural efficiency. If I said, "Alice, can't you become less—how shall I say it—orderly? More spontaneous, more a free spirit?" and she accepted this judgment (unlikely), she'd begin to make notes on a three or four stage plan for reaching that goal. She's been a social worker and is now the human resources director for a foundation. A practical person—balancing the impractical in me? Perhaps.

A little over a year ago, her parents died, only a few months apart, which may have made it more upsetting.

I went with her to her hometown in north Florida for the funerals, of course. On the return trip, going home after her father's, she seemed to feel impatient with me, as if I'd committed some faux pas. A few months after that her mother died. She went back home to clear things out, she and her sister. The childhood books, the saved toys, the letters, including the ones she'd written them over a great span of years.

She stayed several weeks, living in her old home, and she saw a number of old friends and classmates—her best friend in high school, her first boyfriend. She'd taken leave from her job, and she had a good time. I think she began to want to stay—to go back to her youth. I don't think she got involved with the boyfriend again—he was married—but it was a different life there. Reading some of the old letters she'd written, she was reminded of a little flirtation of mine she was worried about once. Nothing happened, it meant nothing, but it had annoyed and humiliated her at the time and she was ripe for thinking she might have married the wrong person.

I suppose we'd become tired of one another. Grown apart? There must be a ton of clichés for this situation.

We talked less. If, at night, walking across our bedroom, I stopped to kiss her bare shoulders at the dressing table, she barely took notice. If we made love, it was more and more mechanical. I felt the reluctance in her body; it didn't really want much truck with mine.

One moves along, expecting things to improve.

I was almost relieved when she said she and her sister, a widow now ("She's free, free as the air"—that enviable state) were thinking of going on a Caribbean cruise. "By all means," I said.

I told her I was thinking of going to check on my father.

30

"By all means," she said.

So I drove away up the interstate. A long haul, and I listened to the radio off and on. And, in the late afternoon, here was Beethoven's eighth sonata, which, for some reason, I hadn't heard in a long time—familiar and beautiful, like a memory in the blood. There was some hidden association with Alice—had we listened to it in our college listening-room days, was it her favorite? Sometimes music seems to speak of something beautiful and mysterious, beyond reach; a longing for something we will never have in this life.

My daughter Lauren has not been good about keeping in touch, but finally she called. "Daddy! You're at Grandpa's! Is he okay? I'm sorry I haven't called before. I've been horribly busy. End-of-term busy." She teaches in the law school of a small university—a lot of little colleges have become "universities" now—and has a two-year-old; her husband teaches too. I understand how busy they are.

"Grandpa's pretty good. Your aunt Sophie is here too. Your former aunt Joy is seriously sick, maybe terminally sick, and your uncle Garrett has gone to see about her."

"Oh, dear. I'm so sorry. But why is Sophie there?"

"I'm not sure. Some notion of helping your grandpa, keeping him company, maybe—she didn't know I was here. Change of scene. Something. I don't really know."

"And Mom is on a cruise. You didn't want to go?"

"She didn't exactly ask me to."

"Oh, oh. I guess you need a little time away from each other, is that it? Well, enjoy it."

The call made me feel less that I was alone in the swamps.

· 6 ·

HENRY

My father wrote Sophie a check one morning.

"No, no, you don't have to do that," he told her when she remarked that she was going to be working the next day, cleaning houses with Wanda Gilreath. She'd met Wanda out on a walk and they'd hit it off.

"It's okay, it's flexible hours, and her mother babysits dirt cheap. It pays pretty well, too. I can do it for three hours and go feed Sam—he's still breast-feeding."

"It's hard work," my father says. He doesn't mention that to some people in town it might seem low class. He may have been a little embarrassed by the breast-feeding aspect. I'd come across the late breast-feeding before—they do it for years now. "This little fellow needs you around right now—just being away from home must be kind of a shock for him."

"Well. If you disapprove—I don't want to embarrass anyone. But you don't need to write me a check. Well. I'll keep a record of this."

I was curious about the size of the check, even as I knew it wasn't much of my business. It was a little of my business. He had a kind of foolish smile as he handed her the check, the kind of joyously foolish smile some men get with certain women they're just getting acquainted with. I knew he wouldn't give her everything—at least not yet.

I'm not eager to cash in my inheritance, assuming I have the one he's spoken of repeatedly. Everything goes to you and Garrett, he says. Some rare cancer might strike him yet and he might decide he wants to pay for some rare cure that would eat up tens of thousands—you never know. But it's true that I assume a certain amount of help in the future from what he'll leave behind, and it gives me a feeling of security.

I had to give Sophie credit: she guessed what was in my mind. "I wasn't trying to come on as pathetic. I'm not penniless, I've got credit cards. But I thought it wouldn't hurt to earn some money, make a few contacts in town." As if she meant to be here for some time? Maybe her cleaning houses was meant to embarrass Garrett, as if he'd reduced her money supply—but this may be unfair. She was floundering, but pleased to have found a new friend in Wanda so soon; she may have been imagining a new life, staking out some entirely different imaginary future that even she herself didn't quite believe in.

"You realize I have to tell Garrett you're here? It's time I called him and it'll seem pretty strange not to mention it."

"Yes. Okay."

I called Garrett. I told him I was sorry about Joy, please give her my love. I told him Dad was doing all right, as far as I could tell. I told him Sophie was here.

"Is she! Is she. How strange. Why?"

I told him she said she wanted to get away from the house.

"To be the one to leave, instead of me? Well. She doesn't answer when I call. I can't leave Joy right now, I just can't. She doesn't have a lot more time. In another week she may be able to tear herself away from here—she says she's better here—and I'll help her get home. She's got regular help back there."

Garrett didn't seem to have much more to say. I asked what Cedar Key was like. Quiet and a little artsy-craftsy but relatively unspoiled, he said. I asked if he had messages for Sophie. "Give her

33

my love. Tell her I'll be back when I can, that's all. I'm disappointed in her response to this, but she must know that. How's Sam?"

"Fine, fine."

"And you? How long are you staying? Everything okay with you and Alice?"

"Pretty much as usual, I guess." Pride can kick in at odd times. "But it's sort of nice to be back here."

And I told him it was good of him to be there, and he made some modest murmur in response. We always got along well enough. In his extreme youth I was trained to look out for him and I did, glad to have a little brother to instruct and play with. Later he found his own path, of course. He left the music pretty much to me and did pretty well in Little League; in high school he wrote a gossip column for our piddling little school paper. He was keen on the girls, and they liked him pretty well too. Then we were both away from home. Later I felt that he rather patronized my wife; maybe she told him to have a good day once, or maybe he disapproved of her taste in clothes (bright), "taste" being one of his almost obsessions. He may have sensed that I rather low-rated his novels. But that's putting it too strongly in both cases.

And we always got along.

Sophie wanted Sam to get acquainted with us. "Tell Grandpa and Uncle Henry what you saw at Wanda's this morning."

Sam was mum, looking at us doubtfully.

"Let me guess," I said. "Was it a duck? No. How about a bunny rabbit?"

"How'd you know!" Sophie said. "They have a rabbit, a real live rabbit. In the house. It was looking in the toy box one day and fell in. What did you do to the rabbit, Sam?"

34

Sam made a courageous effort. *"Petted it."*

"Good for you, good for you," my father said. "I used to make rabbit boxes when I was growing up."

After supper that night, after Sam was put to bed, we all sat in the living room; it seemed the proper, sociable thing to do. Later, when we were all used to this arrangement, we'd be able to separate after supper and do our own things, I thought, looking forward to that time.

I told them about my search through the wilds that morning, and about our ancestor, our great-great-great grandfather. "So he hid out in the swamps and made his way north, and it was a hard, hard journey. Those patriots were mean, mean, mean."

"What did he want to be loyal to the king for?" my father said. "The British hadn't been treating us right, you know that. It was misplaced loyalty, that's what it was. Bad judgment."

"But that lack of family feeling!—they didn't back him up. He didn't have to go with the revolution just because all the neighbors did, but then the neighbors wanted to kill him—was that right?"

"No. But if you're talking about family feeling . . . Why didn't he think enough of his family to give up and stay there where they were all safe?" my father said.

"You have your principles, your convictions—"

"Great-great-great grandfather?" Sophie said. "That would make him Sam's great-great-great-great, wouldn't it."

That surprised me. I'd caught myself thinking of her as almost a bystander, not really kin. "Yes."

"I'd like to come with you on some of your walks up there— could I? I could leave Sam with Wanda's mother—she babysits. It might be good for him to see some other kids now and then."

"Fine," I said, trying to sound enthusiastic.

·7·

Luther watched them set off the next morning, that mismatched pair, Henry and Garrett's wife. A bit odd.

He'd decided he liked having them there, even if it did mean a little extra trouble. It felt safer with them in the house, as if they could protect him. He didn't worry much about burglary, though anything was possible. Death: that was what he wanted them to hold off.

It'll be a surprise, he warned himself time and again. A burner on the stove glowing red while he lay on the floor struggling for breath, or simply *gone*. He never left the bathroom or kitchen now with a faucet running: If he dropped dead before he got back and the water kept flowing, who knew how much of the house—floors and walls?—would have to be replaced. He went to bed in clean pajamas, clean as a whistle, prepared to be *found*, in case it should turn out that way.

This morning he'd awakened early and looked up through his skylight at the criss-crossing network of leafy branches high above. In that high world of greenery, a squirrel was leaping from branch to branch.

Sometimes he woke with music going through his head—the hymns of his growing-up, or music his wife, Ruth, had played on the piano, or music the boys had played, practicing; sometimes he knew what the music was, sometimes he didn't. Beyond this morning's thoughts he heard the strains of something classical, Romantic, he thought—in this musical household, he'd absorbed some knowledge—something high pitched and sorrowful.

He lay there for a while, hearing faint sounds from downstairs of the child and mother. He was thinking of his sons and their mother. If Ruth were alive, she would worry about Henry's return: It had the feel of someone's coming home for keeps, giving up on the world out there, throwing in the sponge.

She was dead before Garrett left his first wife, and he'd missed their being able to talk it over and comfort one another for what seemed a failure in the family. Or they could have persuaded one another it wasn't a failure, it was ordinary life going on. Still, even reconciled to the divorce—after so many years together!—his wife wouldn't have approved, any more than he did, of Garrett's getting married again so soon and to a woman twenty-some years younger. And now poor Joy was dying. Would unhappiness have contributed to her sickness? He thought he'd read somewhere that mental attitude had nothing to do with curing cancer; no doubt it wouldn't bring it on either. He was glad Garrett had gone to see her, even if it upset this second wife. And this second wife seemed to be a nice woman, and she'd come to take refuge with him in time of trouble. What could you do but feel sorry for everyone in this tangle?

What did they talk about down there in Florida, Garrett and Joy? Had they let bygones be bygones? Of course. They sat out in the sun and remembered old times. Did they think of him, talk of him, remark that he didn't have much time left either? He could fool them, of course. Maybe Joy could too.

He could have told her that eventually you got used to the idea. Eventually you knew that some morning it would be a relief not to have to bother with so much you'd been bothering with, a relief to sink back on the pillow for keeps. You needed to go before you didn't know which end was up.

He hoped it wouldn't be a moment of excruciating pain that you'd never be able to describe to anyone. He hoped he and Joy would both go in their sleep. That was the way to do it.

He got up, used mouthwash, combed his hair, put on his freshly laundered seersucker robe, and went downstairs to eat breakfast with Henry. Garrett's wife returned from taking the baby for a stroll. She put-putted off in that old Volkswagen bus—what a relic!—to leave the child with Wanda Gilreath's mother, and came back to join Henry for a hike up Cheeke Mountain.

As they crossed the front porch, wearing their caps, carrying their water bottles, he called after them, "Have fun!"

His own fun was in rather short supply. He gave some thought to it: he stocked ice cream and cones and had one when he was feeling low. He sometimes called his old friend Huey to come by and play cards, and Huey's daughter would drop him off, and they would sit at a card table on the front porch where they could watch for the daughter's return and play two-handed games, Huey wearing his dressy summer straw hat with the bright printed band.

There was Callie Happerfield, though it sometimes seemed as much duty as fun to welcome her when she tap-tapped down the street on her cane to visit him. She'd been a high-school classmate but one he'd scarcely known—a town girl, a preacher's daughter—and he'd been a country boy, riding a school bus, later driving one, into town. It had been a very democratic place, and no one snubbed anyone (except girls who were thought to do bad things with boys). "Not many of us left," Callie said the first time she toiled up his front porch steps. "You need a railing here, honey." She'd married from *off* and come back after her husband died; there was a sister here. Her hair was still more brown than gray and her broad, lightly freckled face was largely unwrinkled, and he liked this, being tired of looking at the changed faces of old friends. After she'd called on him two or three times, he stopped by her house one day to return the compliment, and enjoyed a good glass of iced tea.

Her talk ran to grocery prices, what she could digest, and her grandchildren; it bored him, but there were some things he saved for Callie. He made a terrifying discovery one day, and he told her about it. "Callie, I can't carry a tune any more. Can you beat that? I knew your eyes and ears went but I didn't know your vocal cords went too. If it's low enough I can sing part of a song, but when it gets higher I'm hitting all around it and I just can't get it."

"You don't have to carry a tune, Luther. Various burdens you'll have to carry but that's not one of them," and she began to sing the Doxology, but low enough for him to chime in: "Praise God from whom all blessings flow . . ."

"See, you got that all right. Just pitch everything lower, that's all."

"Yeah. Everything in my life is pitched lower, if you ask me."

He'd never expected to find life dull, but probably that was what it was now. He'd never expected to be lonely, having always enjoyed having a certain amount of solitude, but maybe that was what he was. He found he was looking forward to lunch with Henry and Sophie. Lately he was thinking of things he might tell Sophie—a few family stories; little things about his own history. Henry had heard these stories, perhaps more than once, and he might feel self-conscious telling them in front of Henry. He'd tell her, though, when the right moment rolled around.

He was visited by the past too much. That was something else besides death that these two might hold off. He didn't mind the recent past so much: if he woke with some familiar music in his head, something his wife used to play on the piano, something he couldn't name no matter how familiar it was, it was half sad and half pleasant. The distant past was what bothered him: the Depression past, the sad past. The morning in 1932 when his father had watched the Model A Ford he'd owned drive away, someone else's now—the only car his father had ever owned. At the time, Luther had been at school and he didn't know what was going on, being six years old, but he pictured it later with sorrow. He hadn't been that close to his father, not for a long time—why was that? He was haunted by the time he'd looked at his mother's new white oxfords, her shoes for the season, and said, "They don't really go with your dress, do they?" He'd thought they were tackier even than that, but the look in his mother's eyes, her crushed spirit—how could he have said it? He was seventeen or eighteen at the time. The past pestered him, like a guilty conscience.

· 8 ·

HENRY

Sophie had long legs; she could walk. Once we were in the woods up on the mountain, we split up; I'd driven as far up the woods road as I could, so we were higher than I'd been before.

She had a whistle, and we agreed to meet in maybe half an hour, not getting too far apart in the meantime. We moved in roughly parallel tracks, tramping through years of old leaves, disturbing what felt like an ancient silence under the gnarled old trees.

I thought about her, tramping not far away, and wondered why she was doing this—was she really so keen on genealogy and local history? But she didn't seem the ingratiating kind. And I thought of her and Garrett.

When Garrett had called to say he and Joy were splitting up, I probably had a moment of schadenfreude. (It helps to label it with a foreign word.) He'd been very lucky; maybe this was like evening things out. A fairly (to my mind) ordinary novel lucked out one year and won a big prize against not very stiff competition, and of course I was happy for him. He'd been lucky with teaching jobs, too. Good for him. When he spoke of the split with Joy, I said, "I'm very sorry. It's always tough when that happens."

He sounded quite matter-of-fact, though, not really cut up, and I may have had my suspicions then. Having taught plenty myself, I knew the occupational hazard of women students who get interested in you, for whatever reason. Sometimes they're the lonely losers, sometimes not. She'd have hung around him after class, scheduled her conferences for late afternoon when it would be good to go have a cup of coffee together.

It was a while before I realized that what I'd considered Garrett's bad luck, changing wives, would have seemed to him closer to good luck. I tried not to pass judgment; almost no outsider can judge a marriage. His life with Joy might have deteriorated beyond help, how would I know? (If so, they'd kept it quiet.)

Now, up in the woods, Sophie whistled to me. I called; she gave a few more whistles at intervals, and I located her. She'd found a spring; it was at the foot of a tree, and had once been boarded up, though the boards were rotten and mostly gone. We stood looking at it. "I thought it might be a good spot to do intensively," she said. "Back when they got their water from one, they'd have built nearby, wouldn't they?"

We tramped around the surroundings. I found a piece of rusty metal about a foot long that might once have been part of something significant, who knew what. We met back at the spring and sat down on a log nearby. She showed me a tiny piece of china, part of some long-ago broken dish, that she'd come across—a pretty pattern, sprigs of red on white. "Nothing else anywhere near it, though."

"In the old days they sometimes threw the junk like broken dishes under the house, don't know why."

We sat resting, drinking from our water bottles. It was hot, though we were in deep shade. I wanted to try the spring water but had nothing to dip it up with.

"I know you think it's funny I'm here," Sophie said. "It *is* funny. But Dad Luther sounded kind of lonely the last time Garrett talked to him, and Garrett said, 'He may be getting too old to be staying there by himself.' I just thought it might be a good thing to do. And I was kind of mixed up. Not thinking too well."

She was waiting for me to say something. I murmured, "Oh, yes." I thought I understood how she'd pictured it—coming to the aid of a sweet and befuddled old man.

"I'm glad you're here, though. It might have seemed awkward, just him and me—I don't know. Actually I can't tell how much on the ball he is. He's certainly a sweet man."

"Yes, he is."

"He's funny. He was ushering a bug outside—it was a kind of dazed wasp, half dead, and he had it on the swatter—and he opened the door and said, 'Start a new life out there.'" She laughed, a little too hard, waiting for me to laugh with her. I obliged, briefly.

"Do you mean to stay a long time?" she asked.

"I don't know," I said. "I'm not trying to be mysterious—I really don't know. I'm making this up as I go along. My music school failed, more or less. I guess I'm looking around for the next thing."

"I thought you might be thinking of doing some kind of family history book. Everybody seems to be into family history now."

"Yes, genealogy has caught on." I slapped a mosquito that had lighted on my arm. There was a lengthy pause. I said, "What do you think about that guy I've been thinking about, the Tory? Maybe he should have thought more about what the British were doing and less about the dignity of his little office. But somehow the picture of him in the swamps, sticking to his convictions, living by his wits, makes him seem kind of heroic, don't you think?"

"I see what you mean. But I think he should have stayed with his family—didn't he feel bad about leaving his wife and boys behind? Maybe he sort of got stuck with being a Tory—it was too late to go back, maybe they'd have killed him before he could announce he'd gone over to their side—do you think . . . ?"

"Maybe. I guess we'll never know what happened to him."

"Let's imagine it. He made it to Canada and found some sympathetic people. He found work. Eventually he finds another wife, he gets married and has another child."

"But it's tough, moneywise, he's had to take up some menial occupation—"

"No, you said he had some minor office before he left, so he could read and write, and not all of them could back then."

"True. So he has a new family. But he thinks of the old one. Maybe he's written to them? Though they don't deserve it, in my book."

"Maybe they tell him to come home, but he knows it's too hard, and he's content in his new life. So he stays put."

When we got home for lunch, my father was making himself

a tuna sandwich, and insisted on making one for each of us. We decided it was too hot to eat on the deck, and ate at the table in the kitchen with an electric fan blowing from a far corner. There're some window air-conditioners upstairs, nothing down below. Sophie made a salad using some store-bought dressing, and it wasn't bad.

Dad was feeling talkative. "Find anything up there in the hills? Those folks lived in hard times, all right. I don't know how it was in Revolutionary days, but after the Civil War it was bad. I don't even like to think about it, what Grandpa Overholt talked about. People didn't have enough to eat. They'd go out foraging at night, hoping to get into somebody's smokehouse and grab a little meat, something like that. He told about a fellow that was out sneaking around close to a house and all of a sudden something warm came pouring down on him from an upstairs window, somebody pissing out the window. He was afraid to move, he had to just stand there and take it . . . Sorry, I guess I shouldn't be talking about that while we're eating."

"Was that Grandpa, you think?"

"I hope not. They didn't have much, though. It was tough sledding. Salt was so scarce they took up the dirt on the smokehouse floor and boiled it for the salt—don't ask me how that worked, I don't know."

After the sandwiches, he made a ceremony of getting out the ice-cream cones and filling them with chocolate ice cream, one for each.

"Lovely," Sophie said.

My father looked happy. "Too bad Garrett's not here to enjoy it with us."

No one replied to that.

· 9 ·

Some mornings Garrett woke to justifying thoughts. Lying on his cot half awake, Joy still asleep, the doves on the wire outside moaning and gasping, he roamed the past, checking for happiness and unhappiness and the doldrums.

At the time of their split, he'd asked her if the marriage hadn't been worth it—hadn't there been good years? She hadn't replied; but of course she'd been too angry to be fair.

They'd believed themselves to be very much alike in their bookishness back in the college days, and she'd seemed thrilled that he was turning into a writer; like everything else, that faded into the customary. Then there was Maggie, and Joy stayed home when he went on reading tours. "It's okay. Some of them patronize me anyway—just the *wife*." If motherhood bored her, she didn't let on, but handled it with a kind of absentminded sweetness. After Maggie started school, she went back to work, teaching part time in a private school, guiding her fifth grade pupils through Dickens and other good books. She took up quilting, and soon had a quilting group; it seemed to give her great pleasure.

Ordinary life. It had been ordinary, daily life. He'd put it aside, and it seemed an age ago. Joy hadn't been overwhelmingly sociable. She'd rejected her small-town, Baptist upbringing, and yet she seemed stuck with it. "No, I don't know how to do anything," she said, meaning tennis and golf; she was not even much of a swimmer. When he said, "Let's give a party, a nice little cocktail party," she was likely to say, "Must we?" though in the end she'd agree. What did she want to do? Quilt. Travel. Put her feet up and read. "It's what I do best," she said. Once he'd heard her saying

45

to a friend over the phone, "Isn't it great when they're all out of the house and you can settle down and read!" *All!* Himself and Maggie! Beyond that, she said she loved their late evening talks over tea or chocolate, after he knocked off work.

There'd been a sports banquet when Maggie was in junior high. He must have been off giving a reading—out of town, anyway, or otherwise busy. Joy said, "I sat beside this very nice man—an electrician. And he talked about his kids. His family—that was really the most important thing in his life. And I wondered how it would be, married to somebody like that." She was half-teasing, half-not; a kind of daring in her smile made him think not. He said, "D'you ask him how many books he read last year? You'd be bored out of your skull," and they both laughed. "You're right." And yet she had those rosy pictures of other lives—imagined lives. Some schoolgirl dream of their sharing every moment?

You couldn't expect too much. You had to get used to the things in your spouse you didn't understand, and the things your spouse would never understand about you, never see, never care about. Even when it seemed unfair. With romance, there was the erosive effect of everyday familiarity; the comfort of the customary had to replace it. Then something new dazzled you, and the customary seemed unbearably dull.

A week or two before they split up, he'd asked to read her a page or two of the novel he was at work on. Nothing wrong with that; they would surely stay friends after the split.

"I want to know if this dialogue sounds right," he said. It was a couple of teenagers talking, getting acquainted, and she might remember more than he did from listening to Maggie and her friends.

She read it as they sat over their late-evening tea. "It's okay.

46

It's pretty good. When's this set . . . ten years ago? That ought to be very okay."

"Good. Thanks."

"Always glad to oblige. You hadn't asked my opinion in a while."

They sat on, drinking their tea, the talk shifting to what they were reading, and then to a couple of mutual friends and their problems. It was pleasant there in their attractive living room, furnished tastefully with what they'd picked out together, on the walls a Wolf Kahn, a Daniel Lang, and a Diebenkorn reproduction. The comfort of the customary!

"Shall we turn in?" she said.

"Sorry—I think I want to work just a little longer." In case that was an invitation. He squeezed her shoulder in passing. It would be too hypocritical to make love when he was planning to ask for a divorce any day now.

He'd repaired to his study and agonized over what he was planning. Maybe it was a terrible and stupid mistake. He'd better put it off and think about it. Tell Sophie—oh, God. He'd decide tomorrow. After a while he'd gone down the hall to bed and crawled in beside Joy.

"We've grown apart," he'd said the night he'd told her he was leaving. "Some of the old spark is gone."

"The old spark! The old spark. Did you think it was gone before what's-her-name came along with new sex and new admiration?"

What's-her-name was Sophie Saunders, a graduate student in his advanced fiction-writing course. She would knock on his office door and say, "Hi, Mr. O., can I come in a minute?" She'd want to tell him how much she loved the reading he'd recommended.

"'At the Crossroads'—what a beautiful story. I hadn't heard of that man before, except for the book about Custer." She was reading Chekhov's journal. Everything was beautiful, beautiful, and her smile was the most beautiful of all. "I don't suppose you have time to go for a cup of coffee?" He would feel younger and very cheerful. There was a ringing confidence in this tall young woman. He saw that he was spending a lot of time thinking of ways to describe her. He thought of what he wanted her to read: They needed to know the same things, to share them. She came in his door and they smiled at one another, and he felt they'd known one another forever; each intuited the other's depths. For him it was an infusion of spirit.

The crazy notion of trying to explain it to Joy—the amazement of it—came to him more than once; he longed to tell her all about Sophie. He mentioned her only once back in the ordinary days. "One of my students had some bad luck. She was out running with her dog—he'd always run unleashed, no problem—but this time he saw something, she thinks it was a dog in a car, and he bounded into the street and got killed. She can't mention it without crying, poor girl."

"Unleashed along a busy street?" Joy said. "That's criminal negligence."

"Sure, it was foolish," he said. But he hadn't liked her hard tone. Poor Sophie had been naïve, but she was suffering for it.

How could Joy understand this new delight, delight in that young body that wanted him? He imagined his hands sliding down its soft contours, feeling it quicken under his touch, his hand guided to her secret places. Lying on the cot by Joy's bed in the slightly musty-smelling Cedar Key sheets, he tried to avoid thinking of it.

48

. . .

Every night now he slept on the cot beside her bed, their hands bridging the gap for a while till she fell asleep. Waking in the night, he would know this was a dream. Sometimes, in the bright light of day, Sophie and Sam would become the dream.

He'd said to Sophie as he packed up to come, "Nothing romantic in this, you understand. I probably don't need to say that, but just so you know."

"Please."

Would Sophie think this was romantic, sleeping close, their hands touching?

The week came to an end, and he knew he couldn't tell Joy he was leaving.

"But you can't stay forever," Sophie said over the phone. "Sounds like it was a bad idea for her to be down there. Maybe you could talk her into going back home right away, you travel with her and get her settled back home. Where she's got some help . . . Sam was sick yesterday, I can't tell if he's well or not—off his feed. He misses you."

"I'm sorry, I'm really sorry. Keep telling him I'm coming back. Try to understand. The relationship of so many years demands something. Awkward as it is. I'm sorry."

"Oops, I have to go, he's having a little trouble. Bye-bye."

The next day he said, "Think of this as a joint project, our joint good deed. You were good to let me come—"

"I *urged* you to go! But not to stay for months. She may live another year, I hope she does! But you can't take on that much care. Talk her into going home."

"She won't live another year. Not even six months. She says she's better here, and she's got this house for just a month. You're

49

okay, aren't you? Call on some friends if you need help, honey. This is temporary—"

"How long is temporary? Three months?"

"Please be patient—"

"I have been incredibly patient."

The next day she didn't answer until late in the evening. "Sorry, I've been busy. I had to take Sam to the doctor."

"Oh God, I'm sorry. What's the trouble?"

"Just a stomach thing that's going around, he said. I guess he's all right. But I'm tired."

"Of course you are, darling. I'm so sorry. I hope to get away next week. Joy's not doing well either. I may be taking her to an immediate care place in Gainesville tomorrow. She's having some stomach trouble too. "

"What's with your airline ticket?"

"I've let it slide, fixing it, till I know an exact date—"

"Oh God. Well, call me when you have some news."

Something childish and stubborn stirred in him: I'll stay as long as necessary. What felt like public opinion—his wife's opinion, the imagined opinions of others—had brought him here; staying on was his own decision. There was bravery in it.

He dreamed of Joy that night as he slept only a touch away from her. In the dream he said to her, "Isn't it great we didn't split up before this happened! That's something to be thankful for," and she smiled.

He'd know when it was time to leave.

Lying on the cot one night, holding her hand, he thought: what if, some night, she asked him to come to bed with her? Just to hold her, she might say, hold her during a panic attack. What then?

. . .

Henry called. Their father was all right. Sophie was there—

How annoying, dragging the family into their troubles, if troubles were what they were having. If she were more reasonable about this, it wouldn't be troubles. "Well, give her my love," he said to Henry, seriously. "If you're wondering what all this means, the answer is, I don't know. She doesn't take my calls any more. I guess we'll make it up when this is over, when I get back home. I guess."

Joy took long afternoon naps. Sometimes he read and napped briefly. Then he sat on the porch and looked at the water. Moments from the past washed over him. The time she'd been sick on a vacation, when they'd been staying in a hotel in Montreal— some stomach bug, and she'd soiled the bedding, which had embarrassed her. She'd explained to the maid, who didn't seem to speak English, and pressed extra money on her; the maid had been kind, and Joy had begun to cry. Poor Joy. He wanted to squeeze her hand.

And now she was behind him, up from her nap without a sound, barefoot, putting her hands lightly on his shoulders. Her touch gave him a kind of shiver. Here they were! Who'd known they'd spend this time, in this condition, in this place? It was so unlikely that it seemed preordained, something that had plucked them out of their expected lives and dropped them down here. Something they were obliged to do.

"Fulfilling our fates," he said, in a slightly mocking tone, making fun of these high-flown thoughts.

"What?"

"Just ruminating on our being here."

She leaned down and kissed his cheek. She had bad breath.

Sick breath. She sat down in the other deck chair and said, "It's sort of my low point, right after a nap. Maybe it's the dreams I have." The blonde wig was slightly crooked, and she grasped it with both hands, adjusting it.

"Want me to get you some coffee?"

"Maybe some mint tea?"

When he returned with the tea, she opened her eyes and took the cup slowly and carefully. "I was thinking about a trip. A vacation trip, a long time ago. I loved trips! A new place. But we were leaving San Francisco that morning, packing, and we fell out about something—I said something about how you were packing, about packing some wet stuff, I think, and it really got your back up. You didn't speak all the way to the airport. As I remember it, we checked in separately, but maybe not. I smiled at you and you went on glowering. You had a way of getting stuck in your bad temper and not knowing how to let go and come out of it. Maggie was taking it all in—she was eleven or twelve. We got home—I remember I said to her, 'Guess I shouldn't have said anything,' and she said, 'Don't give it another thought!'" She let a silence fall. "But we got over it."

"I'm sorry. I'd been under a lot of stress that year. That's been a while ago, though, I don't see the point of dragging it up now."

"Oh, it just happened to come to mind. I can't help what I remember."

He waited for something more apologetic. Didn't she see how inappropriate this was, after he'd come and was staying on, at her request? (To his wife's annoyance—no, anger. He hadn't told Joy that; it would seem a betrayal of Sophie. And an embarrassment.) The good deed's punishment!

"Anything else you want to tax me with?" forcing a smile.

But she didn't turn to look at him. "Plenty. Plenty." But, even as he decided they were in for it—should he get up and leave the porch?—she added, "But I loved you. And here you are!"

"Good. Yes, we loved each other." The wrong tense. A feeling of doom had come over him. Some afternoon after a nap she was going to let him have it, call him names, the way she said she'd called him, to herself, a silly bastard. An intolerable scene, and then she would try to take it back—lucky, lucky. Would he go pack his bag after that?

He reached for her hand. "Listen, we should think about your going back home pretty soon, while I can go with you. I can't stay forever. You ought not to travel alone—"

"I can travel alone. I go business class and get good service. I'm not leaving here till my month is up. No way."

"You have your return set for what day, then?"

"I don't have a return set. I bought a one-way ticket."

"Really! Didn't you think you'd return?" Why hadn't he asked her before now how much time the doctors had given her? He couldn't ask now. "Hadn't you better call the airlines and get a reservation pretty soon?"

She shrugged. "I suppose."

A one-way ticket! And then an invitation to him to come see her.

That night, holding her hand from his cot, he tried to hold back his alarm. As long as she was up, moving about, talking, he could believe she'd be alive forever; here, only the dim night light burning, and her silent and still in the next bed, he was terrified. He'd taken it for granted it wouldn't happen during his short stay here. He lay awake for a long time.

But there was a little more color in her face, and her eyes were clearer, their weariness lightened, as if she were finally almost rested. This morning she ate all of her share of the eggs he'd scrambled, and last night she'd eaten almost all her dinner.

"Hey, you're looking better," he said, gathering up the plates for the sink, putting the jam back into the refrigerator.

"Thank you. I'm feeling better. I think it may be what's called a remission."

"It's my presence, of course."

"Of course! Your presence, and just being here. Being here has been good, really good."

If only it were the end of the month and he could escort her home! He'd awakened on his cot dreading the long boredom of another day, dreading the days ahead. Nothing to do but walk to the dock and look at the old men in caps sitting in their chairs beside their bait buckets, fishing, and at the pelicans, then ask for mail at the post office and walk back home—silently, because she would be too tired to talk. Later in the day he would go to the grocery.

"How did you manage to do the shopping before I came?" he asked.

"Donna, she's the one who rents this—she came by and asked what I wanted, every couple of days. But I told her you were coming and could do it."

They walked slowly to the dock and down its length. A cloud of birds flew above the water. She leaned on the railing and stared down at the water for a minute, then they headed to the post office. No mail. "Maggie has been good with the cards," Joy said.

"She has the kids make get-well cards for me, all crayoned, really quite pretty. Even if they weren't, I'd love them."

Nearly back to the house she said, a little breathless with walking, "I told Maggie and I'll tell you too. Don't say anything like 'lost a brave battle with cancer.' You don't battle it, it makes no difference."

"Whatever you want, Joy."

They were silent till they entered the little house. Suddenly Joy was singing, "And when I die, Don't pay the preacher, For speaking of my glory and my fame. Just see what the boys in the back room will have—"

Her voice was cracking, going sepulchral; it was horrible. He sang over her, a crazy, unmusical duet: "And tell them I died, And tell them I cried, And tell them I died of the same!"

"You used to sing it as well as Marlene did!"—in *Destry Rides Again*, which they'd seen God only knew how long ago on a film series.

They fell into each other's arms, laughing crazily—her laugh breathless, but still a laugh. He thought, This will be like children's wild play that ends in tears.

But a car had stopped out front, a car door slammed, and people were coming up the short walk.

A young couple in shorts and running shoes and dark glasses. "Overholts? We're the Aders. Heather and Will, we're friends of Maggie's—" from Gainesville. Handshakes, praise for the location. "We thought we'd stop by and take you to lunch."

"How nice of you!" Joy said.

"Joy tires easily," Garrett said. "We just got back from a walk—"

"Oh, I'm okay. We'll just sit for a while."

She was determined to go, to pretend. Was it for what they

might report to Maggie? He watched her with some uneasiness, and when they all rose to go to lunch, murmured, "You're sure you're up to this?"

She frowned crossly. *"Yes."*

He insisted they drive to the restaurant. They sat in The Captain's Table and looked out at the sun glittering on the water. A single boat appeared; it curved on out of sight. A flight of quick small birds flew low over the water.

The Aders meant to be amusing. They talked about the drive over. "Otter Creek! Isn't Otter Creek amazing?" Heather said. "And that other little settlement where there's always a lot of washing hanging out. Boiled peanuts at the service station."

"They're good, too," Will said. "We started making up rhymes about Otter Creek. 'He was a freak, From Otter Creek.' 'Do not be meek, In Otter Creek.'"

"You'd have to be meek if you lived in Otter Creek," Garrett said, without knowing exactly what he meant.

They talked about Maggie and Maggie's family. "Such beautiful children."

"Kind of close together," Joy said. "But she seemed to like it that way. 'Since we're in the baby business,' she said. I hope to go visit them at Christmas."

"Wonderful," Heather said, though her eyes had widened. Garrett felt both Aders were wondering at his presence—wasn't this couple divorced, wasn't he married again? And did this sick woman really expect to be around, much less travel, at Christmas?

The food was served fairly quickly. No one ordered dessert, to his relief. He could tell Joy was exhausted; she'd stopped talking. He was relieved when they went down the stairs and out to the hot car. At the house he forestalled inviting the couple in and began shaking hands. "Good of you to come over! Great to meet you."

"If we can do anything for you, at any time, just let us know."

"Thanks so much," Joy murmured.

Inside, after she'd fallen into a chair, he said, "Why did you do that?"

She said nothing, only shook her head and closed her eyes.

That afternoon after her nap he beat her to the punch: he had a memory ready.

"Our Russian trip—*Soviet* trip—wasn't that something? We weren't on good terms with them—some crisis or other. There was that awful crush at the Bolshoi—I got the feeling they'd have been glad to trample us. The woman took us up to our loge or whatever and practically shoved us into place—we were late but it wasn't our fault, it was the Intourist guide . . . That was a funny group. Remember the girl with one blue eye and one brown? Contacts, I suppose."

"You'd step into an elevator and it would sink a few inches—I'd imagine it was going to plummet to the basement. I don't think I had a good cup of coffee the whole time. But it was thrilling—the plane coming in over Sheremetyevo Airport, the trees covered with snow—God, it was exciting!"

Some people were walking along the narrow strip of frontage between them and the water, very near, glancing briefly toward them. The heat lay heavy over the afternoon.

"It was a good trip," he said. "I prefer to call it our Russian trip, not our Soviet trip. Our little French expedition was pretty good too."

"Mostly. Though you nearly ruined Mont St. Michel for me, being crabby, and flirting with Mimi Newlin. Too bad we met them there, being with them always brought out something funny in you. But I made up my mind not to let it ruin that beautiful place, the tide coming in. But I hated you that evening."

I give up. "It was just high spirits. I wasn't trying to have an affair with her or anything. So many unhappy memories! Listen"—he made it light—"why didn't you just up and leave me? You weren't that riproaringly happy, ever." He felt sure she'd deny this.

"Go to all that trouble?" She laughed, almost merrily. Then, "I thought about it," she said quite seriously. "But I didn't want to tear up my life and start over. I didn't tell you what was in my mind enough. You know—you always wanted more. More attention. More admiration. But let's not get into that."

"Wow. You make it sound like a hard slog." He was more offended than he'd have predicted. She said nothing, and after a minute he said, "Listen, let's forget the unhappy times. You've got to put them behind you."

"I know, I shouldn't bring up these things, I'm sorry, Garrett, I'm a sick woman." She sighed. "Forgive me. Please don't be sorry you came."

"Listen, let's go for a drive. We need to get out of the house."

He drove them away from the heart of town, out to shady streets of small, close-together houses with driveways covered in pine needles. They turned onto a street that bordered an inlet of uninteresting water with here and there a small boat that looked abandoned. He found some music on the radio, something with a light classical sound.

After a while, here was a big paved space, the airstrip, a single small plane parked at one end.

58

"Where the unlucky couples took off," he murmured. It would sound less gloomy coming from him than from her.

"Yes."

They rode in silence for a while, then she said, "You were good when I was sick, heating me soup and waiting on me. And you were nice to put up with some of my crazy friends, like Aggie Summersett. And my cousin Leonard. I appreciate that. I was okay to your family, but I could have been better. I didn't much like the way your mother made suggestions about bringing up Maggie—she dropped a lot of hints about church. Why didn't she work on you instead of me? Well, I guess I wasn't too bad—we stayed friends."

"You were very okay."

"And I wasn't always as grateful as I should have been when you brought me back presents from trips, or just presents in general. I remember saying, 'Oh, honey, I can't wear that,' and I should have just said, 'Thank you, thank you, it was sweet of you to bring me something.' You *were* sweet. I'm sorry about that, Garrett."

"It's perfectly all right, Joy."

"Probably I didn't appreciate you enough. There were times when I didn't know what you were working on, what you were thinking, what was the most important thing for you right then, and I could have found out."

"Joy, I came down here to renew our friendship. Let's make a pact not to talk any more about bad things in the past. We're firm friends, friends forever—agreed?" They were back among houses and he pulled over and parked; he took her hand. "Remember this! We're old lovers, and now we're friends forever. Think of that when you wake up."

She seemed to study his face. "That's a nice thought. Okay. I'll try not to say any more about the past, no matter what I remember. We're friends forever. I like that."

All along there had been moments when she said she loved him, usually after bitter complaints. What he'd hoped for was a moment of pure feeling, the old grudges burned away; family love, or the love of long friendship, or some as yet uncategorized love. It seemed unlikely to happen.

"The past purified. The way you said in your letter," he murmured.

She leaned close and kissed his cheek. "I'm so lucky!"

·II·

"I joined the Navy but I didn't see any action, as they call it," Luther said. "Just a lot of ocean. I went to college a couple years on the G.I. bill and I guess I should have kept on, but I wanted to get married, and my uncle had this insurance agency . . ."

He couldn't tell if Sophie was really interested in his recollections. Earlier in the evening she and Henry had played the piano together, at Henry's suggestion, playing duets. He'd sensed that Henry found her playing not quite up to scratch; he counted aloud, firmly, now and then. It had sounded all right, and when they stopped, Luther told them it was good to hear music in the house again. Now Henry had left the room; he and Sophie were alone.

"Yeah, my wife was teaching music here, and we got married and moved into the Brumleys' upstairs. That's what an apartment was back then, somebody's upstairs with a stove and icebox, et cetera. I sold insurance, she taught piano. She gave people some beauty in their lives, I gave them some security."

Henry had come back into the room, carrying a cup of coffee. "The illusion of security, anyway."

"Illusions are good. There was some real security. Life insurance can make a big difference if somebody dies young . . . My wife gave the lessons here in this room . . . She heard the great Polish pianist Paderewski play when she was a very young child. Visiting in Greensboro—her aunt taught at the college where he was appearing. Must have been one of his last tours. It was a cold, snowy night. They said he asked for a bowl of warm water to soak his fingers in."

"Oh, yes," Henry said. "You think that was when she decided to go into music? The important moment?"

"Maybe," Luther said. He felt Henry was studying him, as if to ask if there had been an important moment in his life when plans had crystallized. He was glad Henry didn't ask. "She gave Henry and Garrett lessons too. She said she knew Henry was musical when she found him putting his head up against the radio—one of those big old consoles, you know."

"I expect she overestimated my talent," Henry murmured, then drifted out of the room again.

Talking about the past left Luther dissatisfied: Once into it, he wanted to tell more. It was pointless, of course; why should he want to explain that he'd always intended to do something besides sell insurance? Become a lawyer, maybe; he'd heard you could read law with a lawyer and then take the bar exam without going to law school. He'd wanted to get married without his wife's having to support him through more years of college; his uncle was in the insurance business, and it looked like something it would be good to do for a while—make a little money. Then he was settled in it. His sons had no great respect for it; they'd have laughed at the idea of doing it themselves. He didn't know how he knew this, but he did.

After a silence, he said, "I've been doing all the talking. Your turn." Thinking about the past had left his thoughts of the present distant and not quite as orderly as sometimes; he knew he might reveal some forgetfulness. "You moved in the last couple of years, didn't you? Moved to a different college? D'you like the new place all right?"

"Yes. I guess it's better in some ways. In that little town, well, after Garrett and I got married, some of the wives hated me. He got divorced and married me and I was a lot younger, and that made me a predatory female. I wasn't trying to take him away from his wife. I didn't intend to fall in love with him." She was keeping most of the indignation out of her voice. "And once you have a child you get involved with other people, the people around you, no way around it. I guess I'm just as glad we moved." She gnawed briefly on a fingernail.

"Well. That's good, then. Are you planning on more family?"

"Oh, more kids, you mean? No. Sam was sort of—by chance. But since Garrett hadn't had a son before . . . No, I don't see us with a bigger family."

Henry was back and sat down.

"You didn't go out on any historical missions today, did you," Luther said. "Well, it's kind of interesting, thinking about the old folks, but kind of depressing. Such a narrow world. Not much choice in life. Generally, around here, our folks—they married somebody in the neighborhood and worked on somebody else's place till they could start buying a farm."

"Nobody has a lot of choice in life. Virginia Woolf, or maybe it's somebody in a novel, says we're all enclosed in 'an envelope of circumstance'—something like that," Henry said. "They were busy trying to make ends meet. They didn't have the leisure to wonder if they were happy or not."

"Huh! They could be as unhappy as anybody. You like to think about the past? Think about Grandpa, my grandpa, beaten with a barrel stave because he was late getting to the sawmill with his daddy's lunch—he was six or seven years old at the time, he'd stopped to play on the way. Think about my father selling the only car he ever had, during the Depression, watching it drive away because he couldn't afford the tag and the gas any more. That's the past. There's a lot of it I'd as soon not remember."

"You never told me that about your grandpa before. I like to know how it was, bad as it may have been."

"You won't know exactly how it was. You imagine it as happening to somebody like you, and they weren't like you. Maybe a little bit. But they didn't eat the food you eat or think the thoughts you think." He said abruptly, "Listen, I need to tell the place I order my meals from how much to ask for. You're going to stick around a while, aren't you?"

"Oh," Sophie said. "Could we plan just a few days at the time? I can cook some, if you're willing to take a chance on the kind of meals I fix. I'm leaning toward vegetarian."

"Sure, if you want to, but we ought to get the orders in anyway. We can freeze 'em." He turned to Henry. "You're going to be here a while, aren't you?"

"Oh, yes. Maybe forever." He got up, as if ready to head off upstairs, but stood by Sophie's chair; his hand went out as if to touch her shoulder but didn't quite. "I'm going to tramp through the woods up there again in the morning, want to come?"

"Let me decide in the morning—is that okay?"

Luther felt a very small relief that Henry hadn't touched her shoulder. He'd had a thought he wouldn't have wanted to admit. When, in the middle of the night, he went to the bathroom he listened for sounds from the bedrooms down the hall. What he hoped for was silence.

Was it evil for him to have such a thought? Henry was feeling lonely, he could tell, and here was Sophie, alone. Usually she nursed Sam up in their room, but once in a while she unbuttoned her top and gave him a breast down in the living room, draping something, maybe a scarf, over it when he'd latched on. (Luther didn't look too closely). It ought not to seem sexy, but it might. Oh, men and women could mingle without sex, he knew that; they lived in the same dorms at college now, shared apartments without any hanky-panky. Maybe there was something wrong with him that made him worry that something might happen here in the house, or up in the deserted reaches of the park. That he was ashamed of these thoughts hadn't made them go away.

And he wasn't sorry, the next morning, that Sophie didn't go with Henry. Sam kicked up a fuss about going to the sitter ("No Alma, no Alma!"), sobbing, and Henry set out for the mountain alone.

·12·

HENRY

There was another person up on the mountain this morning, a woman. It was ridiculously startling to see this figure off among the trees, not close, and at first I was only sorry she was there, someone to be dealt with, someone who might be frightened when she saw me. I stood still and waited to catch her eye, meaning to wave, but she moved off without turning, and I moved on too, heading away from her.

I had to walk farther and farther now to reach new territory, and I walked and walked. And here after a few miles was a nice little creek, the color of over-creamed coffee, solitary among the trees. It was a little too wide to jump and I walked along it. After a while, a fragment of stone wall, remarkably well made, and not far from it a mass of small plants with blue blossoms that might have been either wild flowers or cultivated.

I was studying them when the woman called, "Hello!" making me jump. She came closer and said, "It's bluebells. It's a common wildflower." A slim, athletic-looking woman in jeans, blonde hair cut short and spiky, peaches and cream coloring. An easy smile, a wonderful poise, so unalarmed by my presence that I had the funny thought that she might know some self-defense stuff.

"Thank you. What are you looking for up here?"

"Signs of the early settlers. Or the Indians. I've picked up a few arrowheads. I show them to my third-graders. I walk up here with a friend sometimes. We think we've found where the old courthouse up here was, the foundation. It's way over yonder. What are you after?"

"The same," I said. I introduced myself, and she said she was Marianne.

We walked slowly back toward the way in, talking. I found my-self telling her about the Tory ancestor. I'd lost interest in the old guy—my father was right, the past was too far back to get there tramping through these woods—but he was a conversation piece.

"Oh. Well, you know, he could have come back and been buried somewhere besides up here. There were the family graveyards, but pretty soon people were being buried in church graveyards. A family graveyard—doesn't that seem nice, once you start thinking about it? Close to home, so convenient for putting flowers on, for instance." She was smiling.

It was a long walk back. We talked and talked, in the open way you talk to someone you don't know and may not see again— freed from your usual self. She said she was married; he worked for the highway department.

I thought about her later, more than necessary. She'd sounded smart. Graceful, direct—

I went back to the mountain because I wanted to run into her. Finally I did, and she took me to the probable ruins of the old courthouse, the crumbling, half-gone stone foundation of a good-sized building, weeds and saplings growing within its borders. We talked, a little more awkwardly on my part because I'd been thinking about her so much—dreaming about her. She asked questions about what I did, what I was going to do. Then I didn't see her any more, though I dreamed about her a while yet.

It came to me: Maybe we're even, Alice?

· I 3 ·

Luther, in the living room, had been looking out at the sunset. The sun was down now; the western sky still bright, not quite yellow, with streaks of orange and grayish blue near the horizon. He was tired, strangely tired, and he allowed himself a very brief wish for the old solitary days. Henry and Sophie's presence kept him somehow on the alert, minding his appearance and behavior, almost minding his thoughts. But twilight was coming on, the lonely time of day. No, he was glad they were here.

Henry was answering the phone in the kitchen. Luther

thought it wouldn't be for him; most of his friends were deaf, and preferred to stop by, the few who were left. He watched the orange patches in the sky spread and deepen.

"I'm so sorry," Henry was saying, "I'm very sorry," and Luther felt a nasty jolt of understanding.

When Henry came into the room Luther said, "She died, didn't she."

"Yes. She died."

Upstairs, Sophie was moving around, putting Sam to bed. Henry shot a glance upward. "Sophie can have her man back now," he murmured. Luther saw from his face that he was sorry he'd said it. Henry groaned softly. "The trip back did her in. She went to bed as soon as they got to her place. He thought she'd snap back. But she died in the night."

"I'm sorry. She was a nice girl. Nice to your mother and me."

"Yes. I'm sorry too. I'm going to have some coffee. Want some?"

Luther shook his head and closed his eyes. Joy was gone. He'd made her in his mind an ally in the job of staying alive; was he more vulnerable now? A silly thought. Poor Joy. But she'd had Garrett there. She'd had her wish, more than you could expect, really. More than many people had.

He nodded off, and came awake unwillingly when Sophie came down the stairs and Henry came into the room. Outside it was almost full dark now, and Henry was telling Sophie the news.

"I'm sorry," Sophie said. She sat down on the arm of the sofa. It took Luther a moment to realize she was crying.

"Cremation was her wish," Henry said, in the tone of someone making a public announcement; was he trying to cover her crying? "They'll attend to it tomorrow, and have some kind of memorial gathering later . . . When I think about cremation, I always picture Diego Rivera at Frida Kahlo's—her hair caught on fire and was flaming. Quite a picture," gabbling along out of nervousness, Luther thought. In his mind, he urged Henry to go pat Sophie's shoulder.

"I'm tired," Luther said. "I don't know how I got so tired. Considering I don't do anything much. I think I may go to bed and read and nod off."

"Sure," Henry said. He said to Sophie, "Want some coffee?"

"I'm okay." She wiped her eyes and blew her nose.

"Garrett's coming here when they wind everything up. To pick you up, maybe?"

Early the next morning, Henry heard the sounds of packing in Sophie's room—hangers dropped on the floor, luggage wheels. No hope of going back to sleep. He lay in bed a while longer, then got up.

She was dragging a suitcase down the stairs. "Here, I'll take it. You're leaving? Why are you leaving?"

"I'm not ready to see him. I'm going to go visit my mother."

"There where they don't like little kids? Why are you doing this? All this subterfuge, this drama! Forget it." Let her be angry; he was tired of all this.

"Maybe I'll go home. I'll see how I feel when I get out on the road." She started back up the stairs.

In the kitchen Luther was cooking bacon in the microwave. He was proud of this ability. He watched the others come in, Sophie leading Sam; they reached for bowls and glasses and cereal boxes, and looked in the refrigerator for milk. Why did they look so glum? Oh—Joy was dead. Still, it had been expected, hadn't it?

"Here's bacon," he said. "You get most of the fat out this way. Unless you don't eat it."

"Oh, thanks, we don't," Sophie said. But Sam was clamoring for some, waving his arms. "Well, all right, one piece, then. Garrett has some on Sunday and Sam likes it."

"Sophie's leaving," Henry said to his father.

"Oh? I thought Garrett was coming here pretty soon."

Sophie waited a while to answer. "I just think I'll go back home, that's all."

"Ready for a trip, Sam?" Henry said, in a jovial tone.

Sam thought for a while and nodded, crunching the bacon.

After breakfast Henry helped lug boxes and bags to the old orange van. "Think it'll get you back?"

"It better."

Luther had come out and stood around on the porch uneasily, waiting to say goodbye. There were embraces all around; only Luther smiled. "Come back, now," he said, almost absently.

Then the VW bus was putt-putting off. "She doesn't have the slightest idea what she wants to do," Henry said, almost angrily. "This has brought out the childish in her."

"I don't know," his father murmured. "She's young. She seems like a nice girl." He felt he understood her. She'd thought falling in love with Garrett was something just between the two of them; she'd had no idea it would put her here, between places, this summer morning, everything in confusion.

He looked around. A warm July day coming on, the sky a pale, pale blue, with a few thin washes of white cloud high up. "At least it's a nice day to travel," he said.

"She should have waited for Garrett and gone home with him. Junked the bus."

69

At lunch, Luther murmured, "The house feels kind of empty without her. Like she was here a lot longer than she was." He felt her coming and going had somehow changed his relation with Henry. He couldn't tell quite how, but it felt different now.

They were eating apples, Luther slicing his with a knife, Henry biting into his. They ate in silence, munching, then Henry said, with the air of looking for something to talk about, "Do you think it was neurotic of Joy to want him to come?"

Luther thought about it. "She wanted to get over the bad feeling. You ought not to call anything a dying person does neurotic."

"I guess not. You think he and Joy were happy together? Maybe they weren't so well-matched—he was a lot more gregarious. It ought to be easier to correct those matrimonial errors, don't you think? But people usually take divorce kind of hard."

"Who said they weren't happy together?" Luther said. "Garrett just always wanted more, more of everything. New experiences. Change, excitement. If there was something new out there, he wanted to try it."

"Yeah, that's true. And he went to her in the crisis. There must have been some devotion there."

Luther frowned. "They loved each other!" he said firmly and reprovingly.

·14·

HENRY

Garrett arrived just after dark three days later. He was at the front door, pulling his bag in, before we knew it. He came in, blinking against the light. Outside, in the trees, the cicadas were making their steady musical buzz. "Listen to that," he said, as if we'd all been talking only a few minutes before.

"Anything else to bring in?" I asked.

"Nope. I traveled light. When I left home I thought I was going to be gone just for a weekend," with a half-laugh. After a long minute he added, "That feels like an age ago, believe me." He looked tired; he looked older, but of course I hadn't seen him recently, and of course he'd been weathering a bad time.

"I'm sorry. I know it's been bad."

My father gave him a pat on the back. "You can rest up here. Nothing much to do around here *but* rest."

"I'll have to go on home pretty soon. Since Soph didn't wait for me."

There even seemed to be more gray in his curly hair. Since my mind is always awash in lines of verse after those teaching years, one came drifting along: *A deep distress hath humanized my soul*—something like that. A bit exaggerated: His soul had already been decently humanized; he'd always been a perfectly decent fellow, even if, once in a while he'd irritated me a little, really just a little—fresh from New York, say, or some writers' meeting somewhere, full of the names of people you might have heard of; at the same time, I'd know I was being jealous and unfair. Success shouldn't come too early, though; you ought to suffer a little first. It keeps you humble. I didn't think the experience with Joy had necessarily humbled him, but I thought it had to have changed him somehow.

He took his stuff up to the room Sophie had vacated. "It smells like her," he said matter-of-factly when he came back down.

His weariness seemed to rub off on us. Nobody knew what

to say. He'd had supper but said a cup of tea would be nice, and we sat in the kitchen while he drank it. I asked if he watched the cremation and he said no. I forbore to mention Frida Kahlo's hair.

"It was good of you to go down there," I said. "Very kind."

"I had to. Think what I'd be feeling now if I hadn't."

Not quite the answer I'd have liked, making it a kind of self-protection. I was sympathetic, though, and curious about it. "Was she in pain?"

"Not really. Anyway, she had pain pills."

"How'd you pass the time?"

"Walked to the dock and saw the pelicans. Rode around a little. Mostly we sat out on the porch and talked. Argued about the past." He made a sound, a long ah-h-h, like letting air out. "It was horrible. But I did it and it's over. And I don't really want to talk about it right now."

What he talked about was neutral stuff. The big white heron called Spike, who often stood on the porch of a little restaurant in Cedar Key, waiting for a handout—but you'd better not try to get chummy with it. The place had had a pencil factory around the time of the Civil War; there'd been quite a settlement there, but yellow fever struck. And so on. We listened, and I pictured them sitting on a porch, having it out.

At breakfast the next day he said, "Maybe I'll stick around a while. Till I can get Joy out of my head," and he smiled, but wryly.

"You'll forget the bad stuff in time," I said. "That's how memory usually works, isn't it?"

"Is it? Some bad stuff stays with you forever."

"So, file it away. Accept it, get used to it . . . Excuse me, I seem to be in an advicey mood."

"Sure. I expect I'll get used to it."

I invited him to come up to the mountain with me and tramp around, though I was winding that up. He came, but somehow without thinking about what he was doing; he walked along with me without looking around much on his own. I discoursed on the old Tory ancestor.

"Poor guy," he said. "You thought he might have made it back here later?"

"Maybe. But I think he made a mistake. Principles are all very well, but they don't keep you company. They don't hold your hand when you're dying." I knew it was the wrong thing to say even as I finished saying it.

We walked quite a way, not always talking.

He took off a couple of days later. We went down the front walk with him to the rental car. After he stuck his bag inside he turned to us and said, "I called Soph. She's home, all right. She said she was sorry." It came to me that we should have called to make sure she got home safely.

"Sophie's nice," I said. "Give her our best." We watched him drive down the street, watched the brake lights come on as he paused before a turn into the busier cross street. I wondered what Sophie was sorry for—Joy's death, one would hope. And coming here and breaking off communication?

Another clear, hot day. "Not too bad a day to travel," my father said. There was the sound of a lawnmower down the street. We went back in the house. "You expect they'll make it up, don't you?" he asked.

"Without a doubt. Without a doubt. They'll make it up. But things will never be quite the same with them. Well, not for a while, anyway."

Later in the day he said, "Well, Garrett's got a young wife to look after him in his old age. That's something worth thinking about."

I said that was true.

A card from Alice, mailed in St. Thomas, came that day. It was an oversized card with pictures of the flamboyant tree. She said it was a fine cruise, though all their tablemates wanted to talk about at breakfast was how the stock market was doing. St. Thomas was beautiful, one of her favorite places. She sent greetings to my father, and signed the card "Love."

·15·

Garrett drove and tried to think of nothing except cars going by and signs, white on green, overhead and to the side. He had chosen to drive because he wanted to be alone, not jammed into a seat on a plane, and his plans had all been last minute.

All these places, all these towns. How would it be to look around and choose a place at random, a place to settle in and make a different life? Starting all over, like a victim of amnesia.

Henry and his father had been good; they hadn't asked too many questions. Funny to think of Sophie and Sam there with them; they seemed to have been nice to her. He tried to imagine her hiking with Henry up on Cheeke Mountain—what would they have talked about? (What did Henry really think of her?) Henry was at loose ends, feeling sorry for himself, probably dramatizing his situation. It was likely he'd get back into teaching at some not very high level job, some job he was too good for. Alice was making some money, though, and was a cheerful sort; he dismissed his old dismissive thoughts of her.

"Maybe I'll do something wild and crazy, like play piano on a cruise ship," Henry said. "Except they might stick you with directing some other activities." As if he would enjoy pounding out the old popular numbers for more than one night!

"Would Alice like that?"

"Probably not."

Henry had been feeling sorry for him, and that was okay. There might be a little arrogance in Henry, or maybe it was only older-brother stuff. Henry hadn't fully loved his success—perhaps overestimating it—but there was no help for that. There was a lot there was no help for lately.

He hadn't stayed long enough at his father's to get Joy out of his head after all, and as the day went on, the last week or two came back in snatches. She hadn't been able to focus on getting a return ticket home, and he'd had to take over. Then arranging the drive to Gainesville, two rental cars to return, and he didn't want her driving alone. Donna, the rental agent for the house, had her son drive Joy's car back, she following.

She'd ridden with him. "Goodbye, dear Cedar Key," she said almost gaily as they drove over a bridge on the outskirts, past the marshes and a few scattered buildings flush with the highway, on to the empty stretches through fields and woods. "I will never see you again."

"Who knows, who knows," he murmured. "The future is unpredictable," feeling foolish as he said it. He turned on the radio.

Settled beside him in the plane, she'd smiled serenely, as if they were off on one of the trips of the past, heading for Europe, perhaps, not to her last days. The day had clouded over: Loose, scattered gray clouds in an enigmatic sky, not altogether friendly.

He thought of storms, of planes struck by lightning going down, then wondered what Sophie was doing today.

As the plane raced down the runway, he thought of the couples who'd perished near Cedar Key, flying into the Gulf. A beautiful way to go, she'd said.

Soon she fell asleep, and he looked out the window at the skyscape of thick white clouds. How could rising among the clouds not make you think of journeys to an imaginary afterlife?

He'd asked for wheelchairs for her, which displeased her, but she allowed him to push her through the terminal at Atlanta. On the short flight to Knoxville he too slept. Knoxville, he thought as he drifted off to sleep; why Knoxville? Oh, the dead aunt; she was in the aunt's old house. And her college roommate lived there, and maybe someone else she knew. Should he have asked if she'd found a quilting group there?

"I'll spend a night and take off tomorrow," he said as he helped her into the rental car at the airport. "We have to get an aide back for you tomorrow. Call as soon as we get there, okay?"

She directed him through the early evening traffic for what felt like a long way to the house—big, brown, and gabled, completely dark and warm inside. She found the light switches and waved toward the thermostat. "Make it a little cooler but not too cool, please. And help me up the stairs."

She was too tired to call the aide. He got the information out of her slowly, as she rummaged through her bag for a nightgown, her hands trembling. "I'm so tired. Sure, call her, she'll come tomorrow, she's good," she said, getting out of her clothes with frantic haste, flinging them on a chair and sinking down on the bed. "Please turn the cover back for me, I can't do another thing."

"Heat your Bed Buddy?"

"Yes, yes. Look in the linen closet in the hall, there's an old one on the bottom shelf. It's dingy but it's okay, I don't know where I packed the other one." Then she was in bed with her eyes closed, looking very pale.

There were take-out menus in the kitchen, sticking up between the cookbooks on a corner of the counter, and he ordered pizza and a salad. An indulgence—and why not? It was time for one. She might like the pizza too.

When he tiptoed into her room at ten o'clock that evening, she opened her eyes. Yes, pizza!—she laughed as he propped her up against the bed pillows. "Exactly what I wanted."

After the pizza, she said, "I'm too tired to get up and brush my teeth. Find me some dental floss, will you, please?"

When he returned with it, she patted the bed, meaning for him to sit down by her. He watched her floss.

Then she was handing the floss back to him. "Thank you for coming down here, Garrett. I thought you'd come." As if they were still in Cedar Key. But she was tired and not fully awake. "We jawed and made up. A little like matrimony, maybe—that's funny, once you think about it. But like old friends. Goodnight, Garrett." She leaned forward and kissed his cheek, then closed her eyes.

Her feelings purified at last? He headed down an off-ramp to look for a cup of coffee.

It was Loretta, the aide who'd come the next morning—small, sharp-eyed, and given to uneasy murmurings—who told him she was dead. He'd opened the door to her room several times but wanted to let her sleep; it had been a hard day of travel. Loretta had gone to look at her more closely, then come to tell him to call 911.

Those mornings in Cedar Key, when he'd dreaded waking up

77

to face another day—had that happened? So long ago. He wanted to be back there now, on such a morning, making the day perfect, making it count.

Now the cars went by; cars, cars, cars. Long ago, he and Joy had made a game of making words from the letters on license plates.

Had he given her what he owed her? Sophie might say yes; Maggie might say she didn't know. Not that it mattered what the consensus was. He thought, How tired I am.

And Sophie, Sophie—how much would she expect to hear?

He could report all, every word he and Joy had spoken—as if he could, as if he would—and it would still not be a full account of what had happened to him.

It would be a while before things were more or less as usual between Sophie and himself. Still, it would be a relief to see her and put his arms around her, and pick up Sam—the old half-forgotten life back again. Changed, but back.

·16·

Luther woke from his afternoon nap to a terrible stillness in the house.

He'd been dreaming of his mother, a comforting dream; he'd been glad to see her. But now this stillness.

They were all gone. He was alone and unprotected.

Henry, Sophie, Garrett, a flurry of visits. He'd become accustomed to having someone there, inconveniencing him, and now they were gone. Gone, and correctly matched up again.

Music was playing far off in his head, a hymn in his mother's voice: "I will sing you a song of that beautiful land, The faraway home of the soul—"

It seemed unbearably sad. He'd learned to replace the sad music with something else, and mentally began to hum, "Down among the Sheltering Palms," a good snappy number.

It had surprised him when Henry packed up to go. "I thought you were staying on, maybe forever, you said." He found he was a little disappointed.

"Alice wants me to come home. So I'm going."

So they had been at outs—a little, anyway. "Well, years to-gether—that's important." He was trying to tell Henry to be glad he was going back to his imperfect but customary life.

Henry said that was true. He packed up, laundered the sheets, and tidied up the bedroom conscientiously.

And now Luther went on lying there, looking up through the skylight at the pure blue sky beyond the leaves. It was pleasant, it was restful to be lying here, and now there were more and more times when it was hard to get up and he wanted to say, Let the world go on without me.

Downstairs in the kitchen some mess from last night's supper waited, along with a few dishes from breakfast and lunch. He thought: I hope I don't die before I get it cleaned up and somebody else finds it and thinks I've been living a slovenly life.

Dying—yes, accept the word. He'd thought of leaving this world as a little like leaving on a trip, looking out the car window and saying a wordless goodbye to Dwight next door, and the tall purple flowers blooming in his yard, which he'd never learned the name of. Goodbye to all these streets never to be seen again. If you could pretend you were going to return! But it wouldn't happen that way; probably you'd already be in bed somewhere, and they'd be getting you up to walk around or sit up in front of a TV set with a lot of other worn-out people; maybe you'd breathe your last sitting there, while silly people rattled on there on the screen.

It came to him—a picture of his sons leaving the church after his funeral. He hadn't examined his beliefs in a while and didn't intend to now, but he'd have a church funeral. That was the essence of a funeral: Leaving the church and walking out again into the sunlight. They'd be sorry, but it wouldn't change their lives. It would have changed Ruth's; she might not have loved him passionately (perhaps years ago, too far back to know about) but she'd been devoted to him, and her life would have been greatly changed without him. He felt a moment's regret for the grief she had been spared.

Try to remember it all, he told himself. Try to remember Ruth sitting at the Thanksgiving dinner table in late afternoon, glad the work was over—she dreaded those important meals—glad it had been good enough and eaten off the good china she was proud of. Remember the relief when Garrett got home after backpacking around Europe. Remember Henry's first recital, oh, the relief when it was over. Relief after uncertainties—was that his specialty? Remember the first time Joy hugged him, meaning she was a member of the family. Remember Sophie asking if she could stay. Remember everything. So much would be forgotten. So much already was. The fact was that in the end it didn't matter; it would go when he did.

He rolled out of bed, as arthritic people were advised to do, put on his shoes and went downstairs. Just in time: Callie was making her way up the porch steps.

"I knew you'd be lonesome when they all got off so I've come to keep you company a little while." She drew a small Tupperware container out of her satchel. "I brought you a little of last night's casserole—it wasn't half bad."

How about three-quarters bad? Something had happened to Callie's taste buds; everything she'd brought him was either too sweet or too salty. There was plenty in the freezer, though.

"Thank you, thank you. You are the soul of thoughtfulness, Callie. Can I make you some iced coffee?"

"That would be nice, that would be very nice. Well, about the kids, my father used to say—and he said it once while I was still there—about kids visiting, 'Glad to see them come, glad to see them go.' So don't feel guilty if that's what you feel. Of course we miss them when they go."

"Of course," Luther said, and went off to make the iced coffee.

Mysteries

❦

"IN VENICE," CHARLOTTE SAID, "you see funeral gondolas—
black and gold, and a wreath on the prow. And these big dark-
suited men standing outside and some more dark-clad people
inside, and they go zipping off to the cemetery island. The me-
morials are stacked in rows—from a distance it looks kind of like
a big wall of drawers."

"Yeah? Well. That's interesting," said Fran in a tone that said
but not very. She was seated on a hassock in front of Charlotte,
cutting Charlotte's toenails.

"Yes, it's so beautiful. St. Mark's, that's the big church in the big
center square—there're always a lot of pigeons there and a lot of
people feeding them." She was on surer footing here. It had been
a while since Venice, and she occasionally had some tiny doubt
about the details of her memories.

"Yeah? But pigeons, though . . ."

Fran came two days a week. This had begun when Charlotte
was recovering from knee surgery. The first week out of the hospital she'd gone to a nursing home, where several times, late at
night, a slightly demented old man came into her room asking,
"Have you seen Shelley?" and helped himself to her cookies.

There were other little annoyances; anyway, her husband wasn't good at fending for himself at home. She called a home health agency and arranged for some help, which turned out to be Fran, who stayed through Charlotte's convalescence.

Home was a house overlooking the river in this town where her husband's last job had left them—a white two-story house, not grand, but well known to those who knew the town's history. It sat slightly off and above the street; the site had once held a mill, then an inn. Now a road cut through the woods by it, leading up the hill to a neighborhood of newer houses. On the other side an apartment building catering to college students had gone up, a little too close. But there was a clear view of the river across the road, and of the sunsets.

Soon after Charlotte's knee healed, her husband's health failed; she was afraid to leave him alone, and Fran returned. Fran had been a nurse at one time—a tall woman with an athletic build and an ordinary, pleasant face, dark hair pulled back in a bunch; she didn't bother dolling herself up much. She had an open, matter-of-fact manner.

But she was also what Charlotte called "emotional." When Charlotte's husband, Clark, had a stroke and was taken to the hospital, Fran cried when she heard the news. She went to see him in the hospital more than once; he seemed comatose, but she talked to him and left notes to him on the bulletin board across from his bed. She told Charlotte she'd seen patients who seemed to be unconscious but heard and understood everything that was said around them; one of these, after recovery, had told everyone that Fran was the only nurse who'd talked to him while he lay there helpless but aware, telling him about her trailer neighborhood and her cat. Charlotte was touched.

She was going to the hospital daily to sit by Clark and talk to him; once he opened his eyes and stared at her wildly, then closed them again. One summer evening back in her house, she felt such sudden alarm at the thought of his coming death that she got dressed again and drove to the hospital where she'd been earlier in the day; she sat there holding his hand till the light outside began to go.

Fran cried when she heard he was dead; she went to the funeral in the Congregational Church. Charlotte decided to have her continue to come a couple of mornings a week: it was good to have someone to run errands for her if her back was bothering her, reach things down from high shelves, cut her toenails—whatever she needed help with. And it gave her someone to talk to. Not that she desperately needed someone to talk to, the way some elderly people did. She still drove and could get out of the house, and she still had enough friends to do, though she'd begun to outlive some of them.

But being alone in the house too much changed you in some subtle way—or maybe it wasn't so subtle. There'd been a time when she'd had fun teasing the nuisance callers soliciting for some cause or trying to sell something. When they cried merrily over the phone, "Good evening, Charlotte, how are you this evening?" she would reply, with a calculated creakiness, "Well, I'll tell you—I think my arthritis was a touch better today, certainly better than it was last week. But my acid reflux has come back. I was trying a new medication but I'm not so sure it's any good—" When they tried to get a word in, she talked right over them. Now, when it occurred to her to do this, it seemed pointless, like so much else.

"Clark was a good traveler," she said. "He had a zest for travel." She didn't add that he'd been nicer traveling than he sometimes was at home. It gave her comfort to speak well of him, partly because now, at times, she thought of him dispassionately. It was a sad discovery: once the vital, living presence was gone, you thought of people with an almost brutal realism. She noticed this also with good friends who'd died, and reflected that their friend Ted English had been a terrible gossip and his wife a secret snob—though she would have been delighted to have either walk into the house right now.

"You see some funny things, traveling," she said. "Once at Harrod's, that's a big department store in London, an old woman stopped in the piano department and sat down and began to play and sing—an old woman with wild white hair. The salesmen were converging on her when we moved on. Maybe she was an aged star—never can tell. I thought they should've let her play and sing to her heart's content."

Fran baked Charlotte a birthday cake that year. Normally on her birthday Charlotte went out to dinner with one or two friends, had a drink with dinner, then called it a day. This time Fran said she was coming by after supper with the cake, and did Charlotte want to invite some friends over? Charlotte said no; she didn't think so, but it was sweet of Fran to have made the cake, and she knew she'd enjoy it.

"Jake will be coming with me—I hope that's all right," Fran said. Jake was the boyfriend who lived with her. She mentioned him often; her private life seemed to be a diversion she offered her aging employers. Charlotte didn't remember all that Fran had said about Jake, only that he bought a lottery ticket every week, and that he and Fran drove over to the Meskwaki casino now and again.

"Oh, of course he can come."

She and her friends almost always went to dinner early—sometimes there were 5:30 specials—and it was still a bright midsummer evening when she headed home around 7:30. Some distance away, she was alarmed to see three or four cars parked in her yard, two of them on the grass by the garage. Had something happened, an emergency that called for a lot of help? (A broken pipe—oh, who knew what—something Fran had discovered when she arrived early?)

Charlotte drove up slowly and stopped in front of the garage, staring at strangers standing around her front porch, which had steep steps at one end, then Fran appeared, waving, and ran down the steps. "Happy birthday! Come on up!"

Normally Charlotte avoided the steep front steps and went inside through the garage, but she mounted them now, slowly. When she had made it up to the porch, the people there began to sing. "Happy birthday to you, happy birthday to you, happy birthday, dear Charlotte—" There was a round of clapping. A card table holding a bundt cake and plates was set up there.

"It's some of our friends—we thought it would be nice," Fran said. "Here, have a seat," ushering her to one of the porch chairs. "This is Jake, Dave, Linda, Ron, Julie." There was a chorus of hellos, and Fran began to light the five candles on the cake.

"Okay, birthday girl, make a wish! And blow them out."

Everything she might wish for was hopelessly impossible; anyway, with these strangers, the wishing felt almost public. I hope I can blow them all out and get through this without making a fool of myself—that's what I wish, she thought. She blew as hard as she could, and the candles went out, only little red pinpoints left on the wicks, and a faint smell. There was more clapping.

Fran began to cut the cake. "This is a Black Russian Cake—it has vodka and Kahlua in it." Several voices chiming together said it was a great recipe.

"Isn't this wonderful," Charlotte said. "Thank you for coming!" with a laugh. She was a little dazed, not quite over her first alarm, and she knew she was in danger of covering it with too much gush.

The visitors were in their thirties, she thought, and the men were all well muscled; she imagined they drove trucks or worked construction, or maybe they just worked out. They talked to her across the porch, a little awkwardly, saying what a wonderful view of the river she had. One of the men, perhaps the best looking, came and sat on his heels by her chair, saying he was interested in this house; he read the local history columns in the paper, and knew this was an historic home place. "Wasn't it an old inn?" She told him it was the site but not the house, though this house had been there since 1909.

"Fossils in the cellar wall—shells, stuff like that, the story said."

"Oh, yes." She almost said, Want me to show you—but then the whole bunch might have gone trooping through the house, and she wasn't even sure she could get out of her chair easily.

The cake was delicious, they all agreed. Fran brought her some ginger ale. After a while someone brought out a six-pack. An ease settled over them; they drifted from the porch to sit on the steps or stand around the yard, smoking. (Still smoking!) A few words drifted back to Charlotte now and again. ". . . Dude! . . . You better believe it." Dark was coming on; the river was tarnished silver, and beyond the dark trees on the other side the sky was a fading red. A few lightning bugs appeared. "It's so beautiful," someone said, and everyone agreed.

Fran whispered that she'd taken the rest of the cake to the kitchen to save it. She sat on the steps, calling some remarks over her shoulder from time to time. One of the women came and stood by Charlotte, making conversation. How long ago had her husband died, and had they had children? Charlotte told her about Clark's last illness, the Lewy body disease that had preceded the stroke. She told how Clark would wake from an afternoon nap and begin eating breakfast, then at night roam the house, snacking and watching TV after she went to bed. Sometimes he fell; it might be a while before she heard him calling, which would upset him, of course; she couldn't always get him up alone, and would have to call 911 and have the firemen come out and get him on his feet. "Night help is hard to get. My daughter said we had to put him in a nursing home, but he wasn't satisfied there. Then he had the stroke." But she had the sense of talking too much or too seriously, and she shifted to her daughter Emily, who worked on a magazine in California and freelanced as a travel writer; she'd been to Antarctica last winter. Antarctica always made for good conversation.

After an hour or so, after full dark had come and she knew it was time to move around—it wasn't good to sit too long at the time, and anyway it was past the time when she normally took her bath—she got up cautiously and said, "Good night, everyone, thanks for coming . . . You'll close up for me, won't you, Fran?"

She thought that would encourage them to leave. She had her bath, got into bed, and picked a book from the small stack on her bedside table, a Sebastian Barry novel, and read for her usual half hour, propped against two pillows.

She hadn't heard cars leaving, and after her last trip to the bathroom she looked out and saw the red points of cigarettes glowing in the yard, and heard their voices, which rose and fell, punctuated by an occasional guffaw. Their presence had been stimulating to start with; she had a private theory that the presence of men was good for women, and, no matter how trivial the exchange, stimulated the hormones; she felt more cheerful after, say, a good-looking young house painter came to talk business or the postman stopped to chat with her. Though the people down in the yard were essentially strangers, having them there without her made her feel left out, and she was sorry they hadn't gone by now. She lay there thinking of what she'd said to the young woman about Clark, and was sorry she'd said anything beyond how long he'd been dead and the disease he'd had.

The next day Fran said, "I'm sorry the guys stayed so late last night—they were having such a good time. The place, the birthday party—they were just having a good time."

"They were nice . . . What does Jake do?" She remembered a thin face sloping away around the chin, a brave little mustache, some light, flyaway hair, and what seemed to her an insincere smile.

"Right now he's with a lawn care company."

"What do they do in the winter?"

"Blow snow . . . He's looking for something else, though."

"Do you talk to yourself?" their old friend Ted English had once asked her, by e-mail. He was a widower then, four states away, and they'd kept in touch. "I do."

"Sure, all the time." (She tried to take a cheerful tone with herself. "Okay, let's get going, girlie, let's get this show on the road!") But Ted was gone in another year, having foolishly set off to drive himself to the emergency room when he should have called 911. "I miss him. I miss his e-mails terribly," she told her daughter.

She had more time now to brood over the past; the past was always waiting, ready to fill any emptiness in the days. Toward twilight, she would sit in the living room chair that faced the river and think about Clark, who used to sit there with her—still trim but stooped, thin faced, his gray hair curling down his neck longer than she approved, though she never mentioned it. "What are you thinking about?" she asked once as they sat there.

"Oh—the article I'm working on," he said, laughing apologetically. "What would you like me to think about?—tell me and I will," and they'd laughed together.

But the bad memories seemed to drive out the good. What came back were the times when they were scarcely speaking, the days when she thought, I am putting up with this irritable, impatient man because of Emily, that's all. He'd been smart— she could grant him his brilliance more easily now that he was gone—and had sailed single-mindedly toward success, a historian who taught at good colleges, won prizes, and eventually held a moderately important chair. In graduate school they'd sat side by side in a class where there was alphabetical seating; that splendid year they'd studied together in the library, listened to music together in the college listening rooms, and necked. Home for the summer, before their wedding, Clark wrote her, "I hope we'll never be separated this long again."

They were separated once later, not for a summer but for a few weeks. Sitting in the living room one evening she noticed he smelled perfumed, though it was only new aftershave he'd put on for the girl he was seeing. He said, "I didn't want to tell you this way . . . Imagine what a jerk I feel like," looking at her almost aggrievedly through his horn-rims. He decided that the proper procedure was for her to leave him, and she'd struggled home to her parents. She'd never explained why she was there, but her parents suspected something was wrong, and it had given her father a round of stomach trouble; he'd had to go to the doctor. *That*—that, she thought now, angrily, that is what I find hard to forgive. (As if, with all the others involved dead, it mattered whether she forgave anyone or not.)

During that visit home, a high school classmate, visiting in town, had come to see her. That had made her parents even more nervous, for they came from a time and place when men didn't call on women alone unless they were courting. Probably they suspected she and her husband were splitting up—and here already, another man! "We're just going to walk over to the cemetery," she told them when he showed up one Sunday afternoon. "To visit his mother's grave." Who could object to that? She'd liked him in school—a smart fellow, his mother dead in her thirties, his stepmother one of the crazy Miltons. He was married now but didn't talk about his wife, and in her wild casting about for future plans, she even wondered if there might be a future for the two of them!—that was how crazy she'd been at the time. He was gone in another week; by then Clark was saying please come back, he'd come to his senses.

What a traitorous, treacherous thing the old brain was, how perversely it zeroed in on things you'd rather forget, pulling the curtain from the dark cobwebby little corners of memory. Things she had half forgotten came back, like the afternoon she'd swung by the tennis courts and called to him that Emily had broken her arm and they were going to the ER, and all he'd done was call, "Good luck!" Why hadn't she learned to laugh at that, why hadn't she forgotten their argument about going to St. Thomas for a vacation they could barely afford, when he'd called her a killjoy, and she'd said, "Joy? We may have the joy of going to a loan company before Christmas," then yielded, as so often. It had been the best trip of their married life.

But there was the trip she hadn't made a few years ago, when he'd wanted her to come with him to a conference; the disease was setting in and he'd begun to need a little help, but she'd begged off. "Ted will be there, he's already said he'll take care of you, honey. He'll pick you up and take you places." In the end he'd given up the idea of going.

The dead were always right; they always deserved more than they'd had. And if sometimes you thought of them with a brutal realism—well, that didn't change anything.

On Monday morning Fran said, "Well, Jake got cute Saturday night—took my car and the dog and drove off about 2 A.M. and got picked up—he'd been drinking. The cops called me and I had to go get the dog and the car and they took him off to jail. They said if he did it again with my car they'd arrest me too!"

"Can they do that?"

"I guess there's something—not aiding and abetting exactly but letting it happen—you know. That's what they said. Well, he wanted me to go with him, but I don't ride with anybody that's had more than a couple of drinks. Sometimes he just lets himself go."

"I think you've got yourself a handful there, Fran," Charlotte said. "Well, I hope Jake won't do it again."

Fran shrugged, with a raised-brows jerk of the head that seemed to say—what? That he might, who could tell? That he'd better not? "Yeah, me too." It hadn't seemed to bring out the emotional in her, though.

• • •

This morning toward daylight she was dreaming, and there was Clark in the dream, as he usually was. "Where did you put those letters I had ready to mail?" he was asking.

"I didn't do anything with them. You must have put them somewhere."

"I'm sure you moved them. You do it all the time and I wish you wouldn't."

"No, I didn't. Look for them. You'll find them." He found them, and she stood behind him poking his back with her finger. "Say you're sorry!"

She woke up before she found out whether he did or not. What a silly thing, poking him and telling him to be sorry for some little garden-variety misunderstanding. The dream was silly, but his presence had had the feel of reality, and she wanted it to linger.

It was an overcast morning, the sky colorless; a few leaves had fallen on her small lawn. Across the street the greenish-gray river was barely moving. She went to the kitchen and turned on the hanging light over the breakfast table.

She was still at the table with the paper when Fran rang the bell. It was a day when she was scheduled to come, but she was very early, and she came in crying.

"What's the matter, honey, what's the matter?" Charlotte said. She didn't call many people "honey," but the tears demanded something. They stood inside the front door, Charlotte backing into the living room.

"I'm in a terrible fix! It's my trailer payments, I got behind, I don't know how it happened." Fran was wiping her eyes. "They're going to repossess it if I don't come up with what I owe. It's nine hundred dollars. I don't know how I could've got so far behind . . . could you loan me the money? I'll pay you back as soon as I can."

Surely anyone would say it was a bad idea to lend money in a case like this. Charlotte knew without even thinking about it that she wasn't going to. She sank down on the arm of a chair. "Oh, Fran—I don't think I can. I'm sorry. What I've got is mostly tied up so it's hard to get at it." There was some falsity here, but one excuse was as good as another. "I've got property taxes coming up this month . . ."

Tears were welling into Fran's slightly red-veined eyes again, and Charlotte said, "Well, let me think. There ought to be some social services agency that could help you. How about the Salvation Army?"

"I tried them."

"Could Jake help you?"

Fran laughed briefly. "Jake hasn't got a dime."

"Hmm. A loan company? No, they're terrible, they charge the earth in interest." She felt herself weakening. She could do it; even if she never got all of it back, it wouldn't change her mode of living that much. Still, it seemed to break some unwritten rule of good sense.

Fran was blowing her nose—and a look came into her face that seemed to mean something; she seemed to be stealing a glance at Charlotte, calculating how things were going in Charlotte's mind, and the distress had vanished from her eyes. Why, it isn't her trailer at all, Charlotte thought, it's *him*. He's been in court and been fined, and she's out collecting his fine. She almost said it aloud: that's it, isn't it!

"I'm sorry, I don't think so. I'm really sorry." Why don't you kick him out, you poor dimwit—a fellow who drives drunk and probably can't hold a job for long. Fran would say: I love him! Love, love, love, as if that were the answer to everything.

Fran got another tissue from her purse and blew her nose again. "Well, okay. I'll try to think of something. Maybe a loan company, like you said. Maybe Jake's brother might help me, I don't know."

"Oh, my, yes, try him. Don't you have some family that could help you?"

Fran shook her head. "Nobody I want to ask."

"Well—good luck, good luck!" She gave Fran a quick hug, which she'd never done before. You poor girl, you've got to dump him.

She stood at the open front door, watching Fran cross the porch, then moved to the front windows. She was feeling stiff this morning. Down below, Fran trudged toward her car, toward her real life, however it was.

What came over her?—later, Charlotte would tell her daughter it was pity, but she knew that wasn't it. It was a moment when she felt all she didn't know: about men and women and their awkward little shifts for living together—the mystery of it.

She rapped vigorously on the window and got Fran's attention just before Fran reached her car. She made a broad beckoning sweep of her arm, and headed for the front porch.

"Wait!" she called. "I just thought of something."

It was chilly on the porch, and she was still in her robe; she ducked back into the living room. "I just figured out how I can do it," she said when Fran came in. She found her checkbook, sat down at the kitchen table, and wrote the check.

"*Thank* you! You'll get it back. It'll be in installments, but you'll get it back."

"Oh, I'm not worried," Charlotte said, which was true; she had already accepted the possible loss of it.

Once again she watched Fran walk down to her dusty maroon car, and watched her drive away. What mad bravery, making up a crazy story, acting out the drama of it! You'd need a kind of what-the-hell attitude: let's see if this works.

Charlotte got herself a second cup of coffee and sat down again at the kitchen table, but without looking at the paper. Would she tell anyone about the loan? Emily would think her judgment was seriously impaired. What would Clark have thought? In his last years he'd been a pushover for hard-luck stories.

One morning, about this time of morning, she'd gone to the nursing home where he had been so briefly and found him still asleep; she sat on the edge of his bed, waiting for him to wake up. When he did, and saw her there, they wrapped their arms around each other and she felt overwhelming relief. She'd promised to take him home soon; she had to promise, he was so miserable there. Probably it would have been almost impossible, the few night helpers she'd found having been let go. Emily would have been deeply annoyed with her. Could she have managed it, struggling along as they had before, the nighttime falls, the firemen tired of coming out, herself exhausted? She hadn't found out; the stroke had intervened. But surely she'd have done it somehow. Somehow. Surely she would have.

She got up and cleared away the breakfast dishes; she stood at the window looking out at the traffic on the street and the still river beyond. It was strange; though she might have just kissed nine hundred dollars goodbye—not for sure, but possibly—she felt quite untroubled.

The early morning dream came back to her. How strangely real it had felt, that foolish dream. How strangely comforting too, as if it held his actual presence.

The Interlude

IT COULD FEEL ALMOST festive, the three visiting Dameron daughters at home together, sitting around the table after dinner with their brother, Henry, who lived a few streets away.

They sat with their after-dinner coffee on the benches that went with the plain picnic table in the dining room. "What happened to the old dining room table, I wonder," Lolly had asked no one in particular, and Henry replied, "I guess Mother got tired of it or something."

They talked steadily but kept their voices down; their parents were nearby, slowly dying in their separate rooms.

Two of the sisters, Myra and Summer, had come from far away—Ohio and California. Lolly lived down below Kendall, twenty-odd miles away. Did the others think it was strange she'd moved in for this week or two, whatever it would turn out to be, sharing a bedroom with one of her sisters? If so, they didn't say it.

Her husband, Kevin, hadn't said anything when she told him she was going to do this, only raised his eyebrows. Between them there were more and more moments when they held back what they were thinking, perhaps storing up feelings that might detonate in the future. Why didn't he go with her to see her parents more often—would it hurt him to look in on them, say a few words? He'd never taken to her mother; this irked Lolly now more than ever.

"It's a business meeting and kind of a reunion," she'd told him. Her father had come home from a nursing home because money was getting low; the children needed to consult. "There're casseroles in the freezer, and you and Andy"—their sixteen-year-old—"will be fine." She'd been happy to get away from Kevin for a while; he was getting on her nerves.

There'd been money years ago, off and on. Their father had been a road contractor, working farther up the state and sometimes out of state. Here in Miami their mother had moved them from rental house to purchased house in a confusion of supposed improvements and good deals; there'd been a little profit from this occasionally. One or two of the houses had been rather impressive two-story stuccoes, some needing improvements that were seldom finished; there was a good piano she'd managed to hold onto. They sat now in an old peach-colored stucco in a neighborhood close to Coral Gables, drinking their coffee, Summer and Henry smoking. No one worried about the smoke's effect on the sick parents: their father still smoked occasionally, lying in his white hospital bed, white as the bedclothes. He had little to say. Every few days he might struggle to the living room, one of them on either side of him, to watch the Watergate hearings. Soon he would fall asleep.

Sometimes as they sat with their after-dinner coffee their mother's voice would come, weak and querulous, calling to her husband in the next room: "Frank, are you all right? Are you hurting, Frank?" One of them would get up and look in on both parents and perhaps remove a supper tray. Lolly wondered how many of the four children were thinking of the old days when their mother would mutter, "He's supporting somebody else up there where he's working, don't you doubt it." (Was that true?—they knew they would never find out.) Their father had never been generous with her; he'd set up a charge account at the neighborhood grocery, and she made an arrangement with the owner to pad the bill and give her the extra money. Lolly thought of her mother— tall, big-boned, a little clumsy, her graying hair unshapely in a growing-out permanent—returning from a grocery expedition, looking thoughtful.

Until lately, their mother had managed with the paid help of a neighbor and the cleaning lady's niece, who came at night. Now their father was there too, complicating the arrangements. Henry was running an ad for practical nurses. He was a lawyer and they expected him to direct this conference. "It'll be simpler if I give my office number. I'll talk to them. Interviewing four people might be a little intimidating."

Which sister did he think might scare them off, Lolly wondered.

There was the intermittently festive feel in the house, the pleasure of being all together; still, Lolly was glad to take her after-dinner walk in the neighborhood alone. Myra and Summer said it was a bit warm to walk. Lolly set out, hoping each time to run into Tom Demery.

They'd gone to school with Tom; he lived in his family's old house two blocks away, and he seemed to watch for Lolly to pass in the early evening. A tall, lanky guy with a somewhat old-fashioned appearance—no long hair or sideburns or beard, but the same old short brown buzz cut as in their school days. And the same easy, talkative manner; he'd always been as comfortable with them as someone who'd grown up in the same house. He sat in a lacy-looking white chair on his front stoop with the evening paper, and got up when he saw Lolly approaching. He was said to stop by the house now and then and go in to see the sick parents.

"How're they doing?" he asked when he joined her. Then it was nostalgia time. He remembered her family from two different houses in this neighborhood. "I thought you were pretty hot stuff, that two-story house you were in—remember? Your dad had a Cadillac there under the carport when he was home. I think I was kind of in love with you one summer—I remember a yellow sundress you wore a lot. But really, it may have been the whole family I was in love with—that happens."

"I'd rather you'd have been in love with just me!" she said, laughing.

"Your sisters were pretty too. And your dad gone a lot—I probably thought that was kind of neat, too, you know, everything more relaxed."

Was he going to say something she didn't want to hear?—she didn't know exactly what, but it must be out there, *something*; it was part of his easy matter-of-fact confidence to say whatever was in his mind.

"Stella's Summer now. She changed her name a few years back."

"Oh, yeah, I think I knew that. Went in for a different lifestyle, didn't she." They had reached a thoroughfare where cars were passing; they crossed the street, he taking her elbow, and turned back the way they had come. A man was mowing his lawn; Tom raised a hand in greeting. In the next yard there was the minute chug-chug of a sprinkler geysering water that reached the side-walk, and they stepped into the street till they were past it.

"Yes, she and her partner moved to a cabin up north and tried to live off the land. Water from a pump, stuff like that. They didn't want to admit it was a bit much, but the strain—they fell out with each other instead."

"She was kind of out of touch for a while, is that right? I think somebody told me that. Your mother got worried."

"Yes. That was Summer . . . I'd like to change my name back to Laura, the way it's supposed to be, but this *Lolly* business got started and I guess it's too late."

"Oh, *Lolly's* cute. I like *Lolly*."

Walking with Tom, she would gossip a little about her sisters—not complaining exactly, not making fun exactly, but *describing* them. She couldn't say these things to Kevin over the phone in the house because she might be overheard; anyway, she was feeling a little stiff with him.

"Myra believes there's a solution to everything—just find it. Efficiency. Being the oldest, you get to be the managing kind, I suppose. Summer thinks things will work out without getting analytical. Put enough heart into it! Something like that."

"And where are you in this?"

"Oh—in the middle, I guess. As in real life." Myra was the oldest, Summer the youngest, Lolly in the middle.

She remembered that his wife was a nurse. Did she wonder at his walking with a woman friend every evening lately? "Is your wife working these days?"

"Not these days, these nights. But she wouldn't object to my walking with you."

Wouldn't? It suggested she didn't know. Lolly rather liked that.

...

At night, especially, their father's emphysema cough rang out, a cough that seemed to get stuck in his chest, echoing: *Huh huh huh huh huh huh huh huh huh.* "I'm getting used to it," Myra said. "It's something regular, like the clock striking." The old mantel clock with the flower-basket design on the little glass door, Grandpa Dameron's clock, bonged the hours.

They were used to following Myra's lead, ever since the days when they'd walked to school together. Henry, only a year younger than Myra, hadn't paid much attention to her admonitions; he'd grinned and gone ahead and started a fight when he wanted to. But Lolly and Summer (still Stella then) were used to having her in charge, calling them ninnies when they did something foolish, directing their make-believe at home. Now and then they found themselves still deferring to her: "Is that okay, Myra?" When Myra had become a school principal up in Ohio, Lolly said, "You got your start with us! You always had to be teacher when we played school, remember?"

Myra took on the unpleasant bathroom tasks; she spoke matter-of-factly about suppositories and enemas.

One afternoon their mother said, "The mangoes are falling out back, I hear one plop every so often. They'll rot if you don't pick them up."

"They're not falling, Mother," Lolly said.

"Or tell the Aumans back there they can have them if you don't want them."

Lolly opened her mouth to say the mangoes weren't quite ripe, but Myra said, "That's a good idea. We'll do that."

Their mother said suddenly, "Don't remember me like this.

Not sick like this. *How* are you going to remember me?" in an instructive tone, as if she'd told them, and did they remember?

Lolly wanted a minute to think—the question required a proper answer—but Myra said easily, "As a wonderful, hard-working mother."

"Of course!" Lolly cried.

Summer had heard them talking and came in. "I'll remember walking along with you looking for that dog that bit me—you remember? I petted a dog on the way home from school and it bit me. You called the doctor and he said find the dog, make sure it's had the rabies shot, or I'd have to take them. So we canvassed the neighborhood. We found the dog, but oh God, were we worn out before it was over!"

"I'd forgotten that," their mother said. She smiled. "A little fuzzy dog, the worst kind. Its name was Toby."

"With all you folks here, you won't need me, will you," the cleaning woman's niece had said, the one who'd been staying at night. "It'll give me a little vacation," and, like dummies, they'd let her get away. Couldn't blame her, though; it was a bit crowded. The girls—their mother said "you girls," and they were quite willing to think of themselves that way—took the nights by turns, sleeping on the front room sofa. Their father would need the urinal brought at least twice in the night, and their mother's trips to the bathroom on her walker needed supervision; still, it wasn't as bad as Lolly had expected. There were night lights burning softly in the rooms and the hall, and they reminded her of sick days in childhood and the calming feeling that someone was caring for you, someone would nurse you back to health, even though the situation was reversed now. She found she could go back to sleep quickly after the interruptions.

One night her mother, leaving the bathroom with her walker, turned away from her own door and headed for her husband's room. "No, Mother, don't wake him up. I think he's asleep," Lolly hissed, but her mother struggled on, slowly. In her husband's room, at the bedside, she turned the walker sideways and leaned perilously over him, steadying herself with a hand on the bed. Lolly was frightened. Later she wondered at her near-panic—what did she think might happen? But she was frightened. "*Mother!*"

Her mother stood there, leaning in close, seeming to study his face.

After a long moment, she straightened up and grasped the walker, swaying, and began to make her way back to her room. Lolly followed and saw her into bed, then tiptoed back to her father's door. He seemed to sleep on.

Some nights, on the edge of sleep, Lolly thought of Kevin. How would it feel to be divorced? Andy was putting together a life of his own: his job, his girl, his guitar and garage band. He didn't need her so much; anyway, he'd live with her most of the time—or all of the time? She'd be keeping the house, she supposed. What grounds—was incompatibility grounds in this state? Would Kevin be surprised at the idea? He had a way of running his tongue around his lower teeth when something displeased him. Lately he was praising the slimness of various women they knew. I'll bet he says something about how marvelously slim Summer is, Lolly thought.

· · ·

Henry's daughter by his first wife came to visit one early evening. They were pleased to see her, this very pretty relative in a very short skirt, with long blonde hair and a beguiling scent, bearing two yellow roses; she kissed them all, taking center stage effortlessly. She stood over her grandparents' beds and told them about her job at a day care center and her trip to the beach the day before. Her grandfather whispered, "Hello, sugar," when she went over to his bed; she rubbed his shoulders as she talked. After a while she left, throwing kisses. The way their father's face had brightened at the sight of her left them feeling not quite jealous, but a little ordinary, a little everyday.

Henry's former wife came too. (Did these visits make her parents think *deathbed?*) "How you doing, girl," their father mumbled. Their mother reached for her hand and pulled her closer, as if to pull her back into the family circle. It had been a friendly divorce, Henry had said. (Myra had murmured, "Is there such a thing?")

Henry's present wife, Elise, a little younger than Henry, long faced and not as pretty as they'd expected, brought the children over one afternoon. The sisters felt they didn't know her well, and treated her with careful respect. The children were a girl of four, who looked frightened when she was led into the sick rooms, and a boy of two, who wanted to get into bed with his grandmother. "Sure, honey, come on up," their mother said, but Elise said, "No, no, darling, we mustn't disturb Grandmother."

Kevin appeared one early evening, as they were leaving the dinner table. He'd come over with Lolly to start with, greeted the sisters, looked in on the parents; they hadn't expected him back. He smiled shyly; he was like a boyfriend come to collect his date, a little uneasy with all the family looking on. His look at Lolly seemed to be a question; her answering look said, a little impatiently, *All right—but don't expect much right now.* Were the others wondering if this visit meant something in particular? She'd never known exactly how they regarded Kevin—oh, of course they all got along well, but secretly, deep down . . . ? He was a dermatologist, which had impressed her parents; she had decided long ago that it wasn't impressive, and ignored the free copies of *Doctor's Wife* that appeared from somewhere. Kevin was good looking in a slim, brown-haired, even-featured way, except for a little unevenness in his nose; he was quietly, mildly vain. They had been two quiet, shy people taking refuge in one another; when they talked in the family group, each looked at the other for support. But that was a long time ago; they were different people now.

She interpreted his showing up now as a conciliatory move: everything was all right between them, on his side.

She led him in to see her parents, one after the other—it was his ticket of admission here—and he said he hoped they'd be feeling better soon, and patted their arms lightly.

It was getting toward time for her walk. Tom Demery would be sitting on his porch, looking for her.

"Let's go for a walk."

"It's a little hot for a walk," Kevin said. "Well, okay," and they set out in the bright evening, in the baking, enveloping heat of seven-thirty.

Should she lead him on a different route from the usual, avoiding Tom's house? That would suggest—what? Something she needed to hide? She took him on the usual route. "Myra says the trouble with Miami is not enough big shade trees. It's true, you don't get much shade out of a palm. I think the trouble is it's so samey, all these pink houses and tile roofs . . . Is everything okay at home?"

"Sure. Andy's been working a lot." Andy was working at a restaurant in food prep. "Last night there was a platter with a lot of meat juice in the bottom, you know, blood, and somebody said 'ugh' or something, and Andy said, 'For fifty cents I'll drink it,' and he did."

"Oh, oh, I hope it had been at a high enough temp. I guess it would have been, though."

"Oh, sure . . . then last night I dreamed about it. I was working in a restaurant and I was making a fuss to get off early to go see somebody—it was never clear who I was going to see."

"Could it have been me?" Lolly said, squeezing his hand lightly. That was to make up for being sorry she wasn't walking with Tom tonight (and anyway, if they divorced, it would be amicable). They were approaching Tom's house.

Tom was on the porch. He got up and came down the walk. The grass alongside the walk was edged with great precision.

"Hello, how's it going? How're the folks today?"

"About the same. Daddy sleeps all the time. Mother's about the same—hard to tell." She made the introductions. "We grew up with Tom."

"I think I've heard your name," Kevin said. After a few pleasantries they moved on.

Their mother got up and walked around some during the day; it was good for her swollen ankles.

She stood at the front door and looked out at the street; she stopped and stared out of various windows. Storing up the views for all eternity, Lolly thought, feeling gloomy.

"Why don't you girls play the piano!" their mother cried one morning. "Somebody ought to be using it. I'd be glad to hear a little music."

"We'll bring the radio in," Lolly said.

"No, I want to hear the piano."

"We're all kind of rusty," Lolly said. She believed there'd never been much musical talent in the family. "It might disturb Daddy."

"No, no. He'd be glad to hear it."

"Go ahead," Myra said. "I've practically forgotten how to play. You've got a piano, Lolly, you must play some."

"It's been mostly for Andy's lessons." But she began to look through the music in the piano bench. "Here's the fourth grade book. We could play together, Summer—I take the bass and you take the treble."

Here was "The Scarf Dance," and they began playing it together, giggling when they made mistakes, banging fairly hard on the piano, which sounded surprisingly good. At the end their mother and Myra applauded.

"Here's a nice Mozart 'Rondo,' let's do that." When they'd finished it, Summer said, "Mother might like to hear a hymn or two." They got up and found the hymn book in the bench.

"Nothing lugubrious, please," Lolly whispered. They settled on "Come, Thou Fount" and "Love Divine."

"Is this enough?" Lolly said, turning to the audience. Her mother was asleep, her head fallen sideways against the back of the chair. Myra was blowing her nose; her eyes shiny.

"Myra!" Summer said in a stage whisper.

"I know, it's silly—it just brought back a lot, lessons and church and everything." All so hopelessly gone, her tone said. And that was stalwart Myra! Lolly felt downcast, as if things were worse than she'd thought, not quite under control. As if they might all fall apart before this was over.

It was Lolly's turn on the sofa again, and her mother looked surprised when she appeared in answer to the bedside bell's tinkle. "Honey!—you're still here. I'm so glad. Are all the others still here? That's good. That's good." As if nothing bad could happen as long as they were all there together.

After the slow trudge to the bathroom, her mother said, "Do you go to church, honey?"

"Sure." She and Kevin hadn't been lately, now that Andy was more or less grown.

"Do the others?"

"I don't know . . . Yes, I feel sure they do." A forgivable lie, surely.

When her mother was settled in bed, Lolly looked in on her father. She was startled: his eyes were open, and his look was imploring, almost frantic; he gave a kind of shiver.

"Are you cold, Daddy?"—but then the cough broke out, lifting him up beyond the bed's cranked-up angle. *Huh huh huh huh huh huh huh*—as if it would go on forever. He fell back against the pillows, his eyes closed.

"Are you all right?"

He waved a hand and lay, eyes closed, breathing hard. Maybe that was the way he'd go, in an overwhelming coughing fit.

He was so still now she was alarmed. In a minute she took his wrist and found his pulse. *Please don't go on my watch.* If it happened, if she thought it was happening, would she call the others no matter what time it was? It would be better if Myra dealt with it.

She stood by the bed for some minutes, then went to lie down on the sofa. When you struggled for breath, a breath that might be your last, would you want the family around you, watching the struggle? When Kevin's favorite uncle had died he'd said to his wife, as the stroke came on, "Don't bother me!" The struggle might be all you could pay attention to.

She thought of years past, years in early childhood, her father home after an absence; she'd felt shy with him. Had she ever sat on his lap? Maybe before she was old enough to remember it. Later, much later, she and Summer had complained about him in their complaining adolescent years: Why was he so tight? Summer had been wanting a certain expensive skirt back in her skinny junior-high days, and he said, "What d'you want that for?—you haven't got anything to hold it up." Did he have to say that? Did he have to say, when Lolly's first boyfriend came to the house, "Hey, there's some young sprout here to see you"?

His cough was ringing out again. Poor Daddy.

Her heart was still beating fast from her alarm at his bedside. At last it slowed. It was beating sluggishly, as if it might give up.

She thought briefly of Kevin, who would be asleep; he was a good sleeper. First he'd have read some in *Fire in the Lake*, about Vietnam. Sometimes he read a few passages to her, which she didn't like hearing; they didn't have to worry any more about Andy's being drafted in a couple of years, but she still didn't like hearing about the war. How would it be, sleeping alone?

It was Summer's night to sleep on the sofa.

She was the youngest, the blondest, the tallest, the prettiest. A neighbor had once said to her, "You girls got prettier as you went along," and she lived with that easy, unpretentious assumption.

(Myra was tall too, but big-boned like their mother, and a little awkward; Lolly was borderline plump.) A few years ago Summer had hooked up with another free spirit named Greg and they'd gone to Maine and lived what they called a life of rural simplicity, away from the subtropical heat and the pastel houses all in a row; she was unmoved by the thought that her mother was praying for her return. But money and comfort were in short supply for too long, and after a while she packed up and came back to the eternal spring and the pastel houses, worked at the welfare department for a while and then moved to California with an old boyfriend.

Now, her parents dying in their separate rooms, she thought most often of her father. There were some important things she wanted to say to him, some time when no one else was around.

Tonight she looked in on him before she settled down. His eyes were open. "You're awake, Daddy! You want anything?"

She pulled the bedside chair close. "Daddy—can you hear me all right? Listen, I want to tell you . . . You know I was gone a few years, I didn't keep in touch the way I should have, do you remember?" He looked at her, a look both blank and expectant, then turned his head a little, as if he thought something was about to happen, other people might be coming in the door. "I was up north and living a different life and I didn't stay in touch, you remember? Listen, I'm very sorry, that was wrong. I hope you didn't worry a lot." She had raised her voice, for he was a little deaf; she hoped no one else could hear her.

He shook his head, still a little blank.

She leaned closer and took his hand. "I'm sorry for the times I made you worry." His breath was sour; had no one remembered to do his teeth tonight? When she finished talking to him, she'd put them in to soak.

He stared at her, smiling a little. "Yeah." His voice had become high and whispery. Did he understand her? His cool, bony hand in hers was still.

"Daddy, another thing—you remember the time you bought some Christmas stuff for the little Rummage kids? Their dad had vamoosed and their mother was short of money—you remember? That was so good of you."

He stared at her a moment, then nodded. After a moment he whispered, "I need the thing, honey."

She went to get it and the tooth container, dreading the slimy feel of the teeth.

Henry had found two nurses, one for the days, one for nights; one of them knew someone who could fill in on weekends. The sisters sat at the dining table while Henry, looking well fed and well dressed, the sleeves of his long-sleeved shirt turned back, the collar open at the neck, gave his report. He had the habit of lifting his eyebrows off and on, as if to improve his vision. There was a little gray in his well-cut head of hair. When he talked to Lolly on the phone in ordinary times, he never spoke of his feelings, only facts about his work and his family and the parents. Could she ever ask, Are you happy, Henry? Life had granted her these siblings; at this moment she was grateful.

"The day lady is a Cuban American," Henry said. "She's experienced, and she speaks good English." The night woman would charge more. The family would split the cost of it all four ways rather than dip into their parents' shrinking savings. It was going to cost more than they liked, but that was how it was. Was that agreeable to everyone? It was. If this didn't work and their father had to go back to the nursing home, they'd all have to cough up more dough, go into the savings, borrow against the house. One step at a time. The Canadian minerals stock their mother had bought secretly didn't seem likely ever to be worth anything, but they'd save the certificates anyway. And!—he'd found the deed to two lots down in south Dade their father had bought years ago, which would be worth some money; they needed to put them up for sale.

The business part was settled. It was Friday; the nurses would start work Monday. Lolly supposed she would go home on Monday. She phoned home every evening or so, often waiting till Andy was in from his restaurant job. He didn't have much to tell her. "Miss me?" she asked, and he said, "Oh, sure. Sure." Kevin never had much to tell her either.

Tonight Myra had a migraine, and Lolly took her place on the sofa. She looked in on her father at midnight. Before she went back to sleep there was a sound from him, like a throat clearing that hadn't quite worked. She waited a moment, then got up and went to his bedside. He was quiet. His breathing was often shallow and ragged; it was noisier tonight. She watched him for a time, then went back to the sofa.

She woke up with the uneasy sense of having missed an appointment; it was nearly six. She went into her father's room. "Daddy?" He was snuggled under the cover, his toothless mouth hanging open, his neck at an awkward angle—very still, still for keeps. She grasped his hand, which was cold, and searched for a pulse.

She headed for her mother's room without thinking. Her mother woke up and listened; she put on her glasses, struggled out of bed and onto the walker, breathing hard, and made her way into his room. She moved close to the bed and took his hand. "He's cold," she murmured. "He's gone, all right." She seemed to think about it; she leaned in perilously and kissed his forehead. "I think you have to call the doctor—I don't know what you're supposed to do."

"I'll call Henry."

Summer got up. "Let Myra sleep—nothing she can do here," their mother said.

That morning they moved uneasily around the house, making coffee, drinking coffee. Henry came, and they consulted about undertakers. In a while Henry called his office. After the hearse came, several of the neighbors came over; they went in to see their mother and sat with her a while, then sat in the dining room and drank coffee. Their mother dozed off; they went in often to check on her. Myra called her husband, Summer her companion.

Lolly called Kevin. "I'm sorry," he said. "I'll be over right after work. I'll see if Andy can get off."

The care of their parents was simplified now. They could go back to the cleaning lady's niece for nights—they fought hard to hold back these thoughts.

Lolly thought of the sound she'd heard from her father in the night, the not-quite throat-clearing noise. Was it a death rattle? Had she ignored her duty, should she have sat with him or roused someone else? She might ask Kevin what he thought.

There was more and more she wanted to tell Kevin. "They came and took him away, two dressed-up men, very courteous. Did you know there're white hearses now?"

She'd almost forgotten the notion of divorce—a funny idea that belonged to this odd interlude at home. Thank God she hadn't mentioned it to anyone.

She packed; she might go home when Kevin came this after-noon. The packing finished, she stood at the window and looked out at the mango tree, the hedge beyond, and the neighbors' white tile roof. She had come home and moved in, had gone walking with a childhood friend, as though she could bring back childhood and keep things as they had been in the old days, or some of the old days; as if it would keep their unsatisfactory but essential father there.

And now she was back from childhood, back to her true age—no, older. It seemed to her she'd learned something new, something she couldn't explain, something that might become clearer with time.

How long had her parents been married? Fifty years; last year's anniversary, the big one, had slipped by in the course of one of her father's strokes. Fifty years!

How many years had she and Kevin been married? Eighteen. We have a way to go, Kevin, she'd say; we have a way to go.

Double First Cousins

TWICE TODAY MY LIFE was spared. The first close call was at the river bridge, when I was making a left turn. I'd misjudged the speed of the oncoming car and was barely out of the way in time; he blasted me with the horn. The sound spread out on the air, flat and metallic. I had a brief palpitation, a feeling like a small bicyclist deep in my chest, pedaling too fast, whirling away. If there'd been a crash, I'd have said to the police: my fault, all my fault!

I'm an old woman driving a long burgundy car, one of those powerful gas-guzzlers, the last car my husband, Norris, picked out. That deep, rich hum he liked is worn out; the engine has come to have an unhealthy, excitable sound.

But this morning I was spared again. They're gone, the others, Gwen and Kip and Norris; they're all dead. No, it was not some mass tragedy: they got old, they died. I got old; I'm still here. Kip died quite suddenly, at his wife Gwen's care center; he'd gone there to have lunch with her. I didn't see him often in his old age, but remember his relatives with their reddish cheeks, clumping along on stiff legs, their voices loud from deafness, and so I can picture him pushing her wheelchair into the dining room, making his way slowly, or perhaps an aide is pushing her. The aide leaves; they're, in a sense, alone together in the big room of small tables with white tablecloths. They talk a little, as quietly as deafness allows. They eat; everyone eats; there's a clatter of dishes. He rises at the end, after the cottage pudding, and falls—blam. An aide runs over, another is running to the hall, calling. He's gone. Gwen sits in the wheelchair, watching. That's how it ended; and I hold onto that picture of them, an old couple lunching together and at least imitating, there in their last years, a peaceful life together.

I went there to help, after her diagnosis. People said, "How wonderful of you to go help out," and I said, "Wouldn't you do the same for somebody that close to you?" We were double first cousins: in our parents' generation, two sisters had married brothers. We'd grown up down the road from each other, always together.

First, let me explain how it was there in the country. Kip's family lived down on the river. In my childhood, "down on the river" sounded tony and romantic. Perhaps my father, saying the words, sounded envious. That was where the good land was, and it was true that the families who lived down there were old families and reasonably prosperous, even during the Depression. We saw their cars pass at a time when ours sat in the garage for lack of money to buy a tag. And Gwen and I lived in books and imagination: we read Agatha Christie and dreamed of the Calais coach and the Orient Express; of New York, where the women in magazine stories lived, owed their furriers, remembered boarding school at St. Cloud, and received telegrams and flowers. We weren't like my high school friend, Mary Alice, who'd married a hard-working, loud-mouthed dairy farmer, but even with the work and early rising finished a book or two a week; she read them fast but didn't dream over them. She'd grasped something important: that her life had nothing to do with anything in books, a distinction Gwen and I had been careless of. Kip's home down on the river, genuinely old, with genuine old two-story-high columns, seemed to us a romantic place where something in a book might happen. And he was good-looking and sure of himself. She married him and lived down on the river, and found it was as dull as anywhere else. Then she got sick, and I lived there a while too.

"Nothing ever happens down here," Gwen used to say to me. "You ought not to be wasting your life here, Marguerite. Go back to college. Get your application in for the fall before it's too late."

"I love it here," I said.

I went to help. I worked; she worried. She worked some too; her weakness came and went. She sat at the kitchen table peeling vegetables or finding the right recipe in the cookbook. But sometimes she sighed, sitting there at the table, and sometimes her hands trembled; she had dizzy spells. She lay down at odd times, and her naps might last all afternoon.

Her mother, Aunt Georgia, said, "I think it's partly worrying about it, don't you?" She came over as often as she could; she had a good deal of stomach trouble and had aged early. "They've scared her. If she could take the burden to the Lord—I'm praying." I didn't pray; instead, I told Gwen not to worry, it would be all right. I worked, and waited for Kip to get home in the afternoons.

Gwen was impatient with the illness; she was simply trying to pass the time till she was well again. She saw it that way, like a jail term that would end. I see us sitting at a card table in the early November twilight, working on a jigsaw puzzle. Once in a while she would stop and stare off into the distance, as if thinking, *So this is what it's like, being grown up and married.* We worked on the puzzle and waited for Kip.

When Kip came into a room, he took charge, and you knew interesting things would start happening and your life would be different for at least a little while. He approached the world with a companionable intensity. "Ladies!" he'd cry, coming into the house from work, "how are the Strickland girls this pip-emma?" (We liked these little Briticisms.) "How's my beautiful wife?" He might take up the binoculars and look for birds along the river, and point out the evening colors of the sky. Sometimes he'd have stopped by the library to get a travel book full of pictures, or an art book or a book of photographs. He would put some music on the turntable, and gently move his arm, conducting it. We could do these things ourselves, of course; we picked up the binoculars too, and sometimes listened to music, but it was better when Kip was in charge. He told Gwen she was beautiful, but she wasn't exactly beautiful. She was what was called in those days "cute," with a thinnish, pointed face and darting dark eyes behind glasses. She and Kip were several years apart in age; they'd been sweethearts at college, a college over in the mountains, a long way from home; being from the same place had drawn them together.

Those evenings Gwen often didn't find much to say—what was there to talk about? The waffles we had for lunch, and her nap, and the puzzle we were working on? Kip was the one who talked. "What do you think Tenzing Norgay is doing at this moment? What time would it be in Nepal?" or, "What is Marilyn Monroe eating tonight?"

"Not much," I said. "I bet she's hardly eating anything at all. They have to watch their figures."

Kip and I played ping-pong out on the side porch. "Sure, go ahead," Gwen said. "You need the exercise, Kip—you're going to get fat, sitting so much at work." Now I am able to imagine her off in the living room, hearing us on the porch: the hollow plink as the balls bounced on the table, my giggles and screams as I missed shots, not being a good player; Kip's little high-pitched "Ee-yow!" Now I can imagine it.

I asked Kip which pictures he liked in the art books he'd brought home; I wanted to know what he thought about everything. I got him to tell me about his time in the Air Corps during the war, about flying over the Alps from Italy to Munich to take out an airfield and running into German planes, wheeling the gun around to fire at a German 109 flying beside him as if in formation, then seeing it drop away. There was the time when a navigator got them off course, and they barely made it back on the fuel they had. Hearing these things thrilled me to weakness.

"And I'd think, good God, I've got to do this thirty more times before I get to go home!" he said.

Gwen listened too and made little murmurs, but sometimes she had a magazine on her lap, turning the pages. I suppose she'd heard it all before.

He made up word games, such as thinking up expressions with the word *dark*. "Dark as night. Dark as Egypt, my mother used to say. Referring to the plagues in the Bible. Dark as—what?"

"Dark as a storm cloud," Gwen said. "Dark as my future."

One night he asked us what we remembered from first grade, and who our favorite teachers had been.

"How about the most unforgettable character we ever met!" Gwen said scornfully. "Oh, God, all these games, oh, God. Listen, I'm so tired of all this." She began to cry. Kip got up and put his arms around her. I got up too, and stood by awkwardly. "I'm sorry, please excuse me, I'm sick. Maybe we ought to move, maybe it's *down here* that's part of it. Excuse me, I'm sorry."

"Don't worry, you're excused," Kip said. "Want some tea? Want to play Scrabble?"

"No, I'm okay. You're sweet." She laughed hoarsely. "That was silly. It was silly about moving too. I'm sorry, I don't want to be like that."

She went to bed early. I sat on in the living room, halfway reading, and when Kip came back after seeing her to bed, I said, "She's not herself. I know it's hard on you—I'm sorry." He pursed his lips with a little shrug, then remembered to smile.

Kip's mother, Mrs. Treadway, came regularly. She'd yielded up the old house with the columns to Kip and Gwen, and gone to live in town after her husband died. She livened a place up—like Kip, but not like him. She came in already talking in her loud voice, almost taking charge; I imagined her as good at directing pageants or party games. Often she brought food, part of a ham or some stew or a pie. "So sweet of her," I said. Gwen said, "Sure. Partly, she's afraid we're not feeding him well enough. But that's okay."

Mrs. Treadway had a smooth, plump face, and sat with her legs stretched out before her, her ankles crossed; she gave off several sweet scents at once. She told us the local gossip, and stories from years past. Some businessman in Eady had run off with a woman he worked with, and that led her to a man she'd known in her working days. "Stepped out on his wife all the time! He'd go out at night and stay gone quite a while, and when he got home his wife would ask where he'd been. 'What d'you think, out with a blonde, of course,' and she'd have to laugh, so he got out of it like that—but it was where he'd been, all right."

"So this fellow had an affair for five long years, and kept it quiet! It's usually their secretaries, isn't it. Somebody they work with."

"Don't worry," Gwen said with a lazy air. "Miss Bertha"—Kip's office help at the courthouse—"is homely as a mud fence, and twenty-odd years older than he is." Mrs. Treadway squealed, "Oh, honey!" as if Gwen had said something extra-witty, or as if she herself had been found out doing something cute but risky.

To me she said, "Not many girls would sacrifice their college years like this. I see the styles in the Charlotte paper, the going-back-to-school things, so cute." She would look at me searchingly. "Don't put it off too long, honey. It gets too hard to go back." My going was her other topic, along with the faithlessness of men. I'd never have guessed that she thought about college that much; Kip was the only one in her family who'd gone. She knew our family was "smart," of course, but to her that was just another characteristic, like "tall" or "brown haired."

I will admit that what I remember about Gwen's physical condition that winter is chiefly what Kip said about it. "Her dizziness is getting a little worse," he said the night of her little blowup. "I don't want her to fall. Think she'd use a cane if I got one?"

"I could try to talk her into it."

"Maybe if I got a really handsome one . . . Well, she doesn't seem a whole lot worse, but it's hard to tell."

It was the next summer when we heard that a preacher was conducting healing services at a revival meeting in a little backwoods church.

I was surprised when Gwen said one night, "Let's go hear that preacher—the healer? I always wanted to know what they did, if they ranted and hollered, or what. It'll be an experience."

A hot August evening. We drove over unfamiliar country roads, fields of high corn often walling us in on both sides; we rattled over creeks on plank bridges. "The creek's low," Kip said. "Wonder if they're praying for rain." The houses were farther apart out here, and I felt the landscape had been unchanged for years; the farms seemed to lie there in a deep calm. A calm seemed to lie over us, too; we didn't talk much.

The church, when we found it, was as it must have been seventy years before: white, square and squat, on brick legs exposing the space under it; wooden steps up to two separate doors. The people were going in. I thought they might give us hard looks, strangers in simple, sporty summer clothes, not their Sunday dress-up style; I thought they'd see through us and know we were there from curiosity. But they didn't give us hard looks; they understood Gwen better than I did.

We'd gone back to childhood. Back to the time when we took for granted the exhortations from the pulpit during revival week, and the tears of sinners at the altar, as often as not just some nervous teenage girl whose parents had instructed her that it was time to join the church. Back to the days before we'd begun to note and treasure the preacher's mispronunciations and shaky grammar. Now we sat on the hard benches of an even more primitive church than ours, among the kind of people we'd known forever but were sure we were different from; poor, taciturn, freshly washed people who'd sung doggedly from these worn hymnals through flush times and bad, singing about rescuing the perishing and showers of blessings. The church had an odd dry smell, like ancient paper or the dusty burlap curtains on wires that were used to separate the classes for Sunday School.

Then the preaching. The preacher was not young—tall, a bit stooped, his hair at the temples flaring white against the dark gray, as if it had been dusted with cornstarch for the stage. His suit coat hung long, as if too large; he took it off and folded it fastidiously over the chair behind the pulpit, stripping for action. He had a powerful voice.

At the end of the sermon he invited those in search of healing to come forward. "O Lord, we call on the healing power of Jesus of Nazareth—"

All around the church people rose, as if dutifully. Some of them were helping other people to their feet. A young couple went up the aisle, a pink blanket trailing from the baby in the man's arms; a middle-aged man in a short-sleeved white shirt helped an old woman whose hip moved with an odd rotating motion.

"The baby's sickly," the woman beside me whispered, without looking at me. I nodded. And I saw with uneasy surprise that my cousin was getting to her feet.

From the back of the church a woman shouted, "Bless the Lord, bless his holy name!"

"What's the matter with her?" the woman whispered.

"Multiple sclerosis. They *say*." The woman nodded wisely at "they say." What did *they* know! And I was glad for this whispering woman, for I felt left alone as Gwen and Kip made their way up the aisle.

Up the aisle! At their wedding they'd walked up the aisle together. A simple wedding, at Christmastime. Gwen had planned it, and might have modeled it on a wedding she'd read about long ago in *The Charlotte Observer*: in adolescence she'd kept a scrap-book of her favorite weddings from the Sunday paper. Poinsettias and holly, red candles flickering, Gwen in a white velveteen dress her mother had made; her parents snuffling off and on. "Bet it makes you think about when you're gonna get married," one of my cousins said afterward, but it didn't. How could I ever match *this* wedding? I imagined them lounging in each other's arms, by firelight, dreamy and perfect, as in a magazine illustration.

That early evening in the country church the preacher was praying over the old woman with the bad hip. Kip and Gwen came next. Kip murmured something to the preacher, and they knelt at the altar rail. The preacher's voice went a little softer. "Oh, Lord, grant us tonight thy merciful healing power . . ."

I closed my eyes and tried to shift my thoughts to something else. But tears had come; I was moved against my will. The woman beside me whispered, "I'll pray for her."

In the car on the way home Gwen was jolly. "What a voice he had! That's the secret, their voices. The power of sugges-tion, it's like hypnosis. It can work sometimes. Actually I feel better already." She pretended she was joking, but I knew her; she wasn't joking. I should have understood then what she was going through.

Kip and I went blackberry picking one Saturday that summer. "We'll make you a pie," I said to Gwen. "You used to say it was your favorite." The blackberries grew wild along ditches and the railroad right-of-way. "I'm taking Kip along to keep off the snakes."

"Ah, Kip the snake killer," Kip said. "Let's hope we don't step on any."

"You don't need to do that. I don't need a pie," Gwen said. She looked positively distressed. "You'll get a lot of redbug bites, that's all. You don't need to!"

"They're just going to waste," I said. "We won't be gone long."

A beautiful hot day, the berries at their peak. I was happy to go tramping off with Kip. I don't remember what we talked about, maybe about picking huckleberries in the woods in the spring; maybe I told him about the time we'd found some frog legs in a brown paper bag by the side of the road when we were out looking for huckleberries. Whatever we talked about, it probably wasn't Gwen. I remember that she seemed somewhat sulky the rest of the day.

"You've let another fall go by, honey," Mrs. Treadway said to me in the kitchen, where she was stacking her gifts of food in the refrigerator. "When do you have to get your application in for the next year? Is it in the spring?"

"She needs me," I said. "We're *compatible*. She doesn't want some boring workhorse. It's pretty dull for her down here."

She raised her eyebrows. "Why's it so dull? She's got Kip. And people come." They did, occasionally, old married classmates, and in between keeping their kids out of mischief, they told her about having a TV set now, and about other people's doctors and illnesses. "Well, I think you better think about the future. It's more important than you may know. I've seen it happen . . ."

She didn't say what she'd seen happen. I couldn't understand this obsession. Maybe she was a little batty. I could see her thinking about it half the time when she looked at me: You've got to go, you've got to go.

. . .

My boyfriend, Norris, wrote from college, and conscientiously reported his double dates ("to do a friend a favor"); according to him, he was indifferent to all the girls he dated. "She was a hard looker, I can tell you." He came home on weekends and took me out. "A real nice family," he'd say, speaking of Kip's folks as we drove away from the house. "One of the pioneer families, you know, they've had that mill forever. It's *historic*." We held hands in the movies and kissed goodnight. I felt that we were like some old married couple, comfortable, rather sure of one another, and that Kip and Gwen, back in the house, were the young lovers, still full of unresolved passion, still working things out. I'd wonder what they'd been saying or doing in my absence.

One morning in December, after Kip left for work, Gwen and I took off. She wanted to go somewhere, and there was a second car, the one she'd used in her job as a reading consultant for the county schools. We went out through the still chill morning, past the limp and withered vegetation of the yard, silvered with frost, and she headed for the driver's side. "It's okay. I feel pretty good today."

We went up our county road to the paved road and turned south through sparsely settled country, once the country of big "plantations," now too far from town for easy access to a job. A woman sweeping a front porch stopped and stared at us, and her dog ran out, eager for a car to chase. Down to the river bridge, a kingfisher high on a wire, and then we were in the next county. Farm fields and small poor houses; little towns with one or two fine old houses and then more fields; defunct one-room roadside stores, side roads with hand-lettered signs for fruits long out of season. I couldn't help wishing Kip was along.

"Isn't this wonderful! You feel so free out on the road," Gwen cried. "We could go anywhere. We could *disappear*."

"We don't have enough clothes along." I wondered if she'd brought extra money. "Anyway, we didn't tell Kip."

She made a dismissive noise.

"He's nice," she said thoughtfully, as if someone had questioned it—a funny thing to say about your husband. "But what's he in that dumb job at the courthouse for? He likes it that they vote him in, but of course they will, as long as he's a Democrat. And partly because he's good looking and smiles a lot. They may even vote for him partly because they know I'm sick! Why didn't he decide to do something interesting? He thinks he knows more than he does. Forrest and Clay"—his brothers, getting rich at their mill farther down the river—"they're nice, but what are they interested in except work and making money?"

When you begin to think how he is like the rest of his family, watch out. "You're crazy about him," I said lightly, to get her off this jag. Anyway, it had to be true; anyone would love Kip.

"When something like this hits you, you realize you've got just one life; till then you know it but don't *realize* it."

I felt sympathy, of course; of course I did. But she talked as if being sick had given her some superior wisdom; it had set her apart. (She was a little spoiled, my mother always said—the only child of aging parents.) And why had she picked him in the first place? We took getting married for granted, of course, it was simply what you did back then; but beyond that, why? Sex, I suppose, the need that draws men and women together—need overlooks so much. But I didn't want to look at that then, not *theirs*, I mean.

"You're getting better, you'll get your health back. Look, here's the South Carolina line."

I thought she'd want to turn back then, but, if anything, she stepped on the gas. Being in a new state made us farther away than ever. Were we ever going back?

We had lunch in a small-town hotel. There among the white cloths and quiet waiters, we were different; you might have thought we were two footloose girls off on a trip, going who knew where. We debated the choice of dessert, and took the banana pudding. Then she drove on. In another small town, she suddenly turned into the driveway of a big house with green striped awnings. "I've always wanted a house with awnings!" she said, turning the car around rather carelessly, and stopping. "You can drive now." I was relieved when, in late afternoon, I turned into the yard.

"We took a ride today," she said to Kip that night. "We drove down to South Carolina." Not quite challengingly.

"Oh! Well. Good. I hope you had fun." He looked not so much baffled as tired. He didn't ask who'd done the driving, or how far we went; he didn't ask one single thing.

I suppose she was getting worse. I suppose I was denying it, I suppose that's why I don't remember the specifics. I suppose. She was using the cane he'd bought her, a handsome black one with a brass head; she visited the doctors in Charlotte from time to time, but medical science was not then what it is today, of course.

The night everything fell apart, we'd gone to a movie.

"I didn't like that movie," Gwen said on the way home. She didn't get out much, so she must have wanted the evening to be perfect. "Why'd we go to that movie?"

"It wasn't too bad, was it?" Kip said. "Lana Turner was very beautiful."

The wrong thing to say, maybe, considering Gwen's mood. We were passing some woods, and I said, "Hey, did you hear the owls last night?"

"Yeah, wonderful," Kip said.

"I didn't! I didn't hear them, why didn't you come tell me?" Gwen said in an anguished voice. Was she going to burst into tears? Kip patted her arm, and we were silent for a while.

Back at the house, some of their old college yearbooks were spread out in the living room. She'd been looking at them for a day or two, and after we settled down with some tea, she picked one of them up and riffled through it.

"Here's Jim Dellinger, remember him? I had quite a crush on him, and he finally asked me out. We went to a wonderful concert together. And a picnic—a wonderful picnic. And some other things."

"I guess that was before we got together, dearie," Kip said.

"Yes. You don't remember him at all? A good-looking guy, and not a bit stuck up. We went to *The Messiah* together at Christmas, it was so lovely, the choir in red robes—I was so moved, I nearly squeezed his hand to pieces. A swell guy."

"I'm sorry things didn't work out for you and Mr. Dellinger," Kip said, trying for lightness.

That would surely wake her up. But no. "Yes. If I'd married him ... Change one thing and everything else is different—isn't that true? I mean, think about it, how could it work any other way?"

It was stubborn of Kip to let a silence fall. I wanted to sink through the floor, I wanted to sneak out of the room. That was what I ought to have done, instead of saying, "It's not Kip's fault you're sick! You think it's easy for him?" It was automatic, like an in-law courtesy, taking up for the visitor.

Gwen turned a hollow look on me. "What do you know about it? Well. There's no love like your first love. Or is there? If I were a thousand miles away from here, I'd be well. I'd start over, nobody I knew, me and my cane, I swear I could make it, oh God." She wasn't crying, though. Hard as nails!

Something had touched Kip, and he went over and tried to put his arms around her. "It's all right, hon, you're going to be okay."

She got up and leaned on her cane; she was going to her room. "I can't stand it here any longer. I'm going to pray tonight that I die. I don't know what to pray for, for you two." She was balanced on the cane and starting for her room.

"Listen—" Kip moved along beside her. He followed her down the hall.

I couldn't read or look at picture books or anything else. I sat there, waiting for my heart to stop pounding.

Kip didn't return. I went to my room and got ready for bed, though it was early, thinking to read in bed. But after a while I couldn't stay there any longer, and I put on my robe and went down the hall, tiptoeing. I tiptoed to his room and tapped very lightly on his door.

I shouldn't have tiptoed. I shouldn't have tapped on his door.

He came to the door in his pajamas and said, "Wait a minute," but I stepped in, so she wouldn't hear us; I didn't want to disturb her, and that is true. I felt for her, I felt for her as much as I could in my young foolishness, but I felt for him too, and I stepped into his room while he was getting his bathrobe on, and said, "Kip, it's awful. I know she doesn't mean it. It's the disease." And I put my arms around him because I *felt* for him, and that's all. We held each other a while, we *needed* to, I think anyone could understand that. I don't suppose it was the only time we hugged. It's been a long time since then; I suppose there are things I've forgotten. Which is my privilege.

College catalogs came in the mail that spring. "Yes, I sent for them," Gwen said. She seemed to be in good spirits. "We can't have you wasting your life here. Pretty soon it'll be too late to ever go back."

Years later, I wondered what they said about me afterward. I think of her often now.

When Norris was sick for the last time, I wanted to say to the rest of the world: drop what you're doing, everybody, let the whole world get busy right now and keep this from happening! The doctors and nurses and friends and neighbors were resigned— how could that be? How could the postman come as usual, the people in cars drive past indifferently? A man was dying, about to be taken away for once and all. Call the authorities—this was our last chance, our final opportunity! For Norris, whom I hadn't always treasured.

That must have been what she felt, contemplating her own life.

Of course, Gwen didn't die young. Three or four years after I left, the disease went into remission. It was a long time before she went to a care center, and then it was because they couldn't get good help, my mother wrote.

"He wasn't a skirt chaser," Gwen said, "but he was drawn to women, it was just the way he was." She said it casually, with an easy, authoritative superiority.

I didn't want to talk about Kip. The past can almost startle me now; that's what time does. Kip: a nice guy, fascinating in my

younger days; a guy I'd had a crush on. The morning after she'd
been so angry and wanted to take her cane and leave, could I have
said, "Nothing has ever happened between him and me, Gwen"?
She might have said, "What on earth are you talking about?"—
offended at the presumption, offended enough to change things
between us forever. Which, to a great extent, happened anyway.

Here in the care center, she was looking good. Her face hadn't
spread or gone puffy like so many of the faces around us. There
was a little indentation in each cheek, as if the sculptor had pressed
a fingertip there. She talked slowly, with an equanimity missing
in the old days.

I'd been back before; I'd come back and hugged her and hugged
Kip too; later I'd visited her after he was gone. Sometimes Norris
was along on my visits, sometimes not. This was my first time
back in some time. Norris had been poorly for years before he
died, and I hadn't wanted to leave him alone out in California,
the kids grown and gone.

"It was just the way Kip was. He *responded* to women," she said.
"I wonder if people gossiped about him and some of the women
that stayed with me." Was she asking me? People had been careful not to let anything slip to her, or else they'd hinted and she'd
tuned them out. Then again, maybe nothing had happened, ever.
I'd more or less refused to believe the gossip my mother reported
about him and Ramelle Oliver. She wouldn't have been his type,
with her showy sweetness, her plump legs in nurses' oxfords, her
face going matronly early because of a budding double chin. The
rumors made me almost angry.

"Two women and a man in a house—people gossip, they just
will," I said. I wished that I could keep from wondering if she and
Kip had gone on sleeping together during those years.

"He died right here, in the dining room."

"I know."

"I loved him, of course I loved him." Was she wrapping up the bothersome past in a neat package to file it away? "He did get on my nerves. Playing ping-pong out on the porch with whatever girl was there, kidding around, putting his arm around her shoulders—I was sensitive. Too sensitive." Was she remembering Ramelle, or me? "After all, I was sick! I felt *insecure*. I lived with uncertainty, whether I ought to have or not." A fretful look crossed her face; it was something she wanted to say, but not necessarily to me.

"I had a crush on him. A silly schoolgirl crush." Time to pull it all out in the open and get it over. Probably thinking about Kip all the time had had something to do with my marrying Norris as soon as I'd finished the next year at college.

"Did you!" Her manner was artificial and dismissive. Maybe with that illness you forgot things, though I'd never noticed it. More likely you harbored them. "Well, you weren't the only one . . . I wish Mal would stop by. Malcolm. I'd like for you to meet him. We read poems to each other. Do you remember 'The Night Has a Thousand Eyes'? Some of the ones we used to love. 'Who Loves the Rain' . . . Maybe they're out of style, but I love them. I can imagine I'm fifteen again!" She laughed.

"Wonderful. That's wonderful."

Mal didn't show up, though, and after a while I kissed her goodbye. "Oh, Gwen, it's so great to see you. I wish we hadn't lived so far apart, I've missed you so much!" I was afraid tears would come to my eyes; really, I hadn't let myself think, till I saw her again, how very much I *had* missed her, how she appeared in all my memories of the past, and in my dreams more nights than I could count. She smiled politely, murmured, "I know." Without much feeling, so far as I could tell.

It might have been something else, the illness, say, that had thrown up this wall between her and me. And we were so much alike!—two people who had felt our way through life half-blindly, at the mercy of our dream worlds.

After people die, you think: I should have managed it somehow. That is what you always think.

The past can be all squared away in your mind, too long ago to think about at all, then something happens some gray day, and everything falls into disorder, like a room shaken by an earthquake. The books all in a heap on the floor, the china jumbled and cracked in the cupboards.

Today there was a smell of ashes in the house: it rained all week till today, and a little rain gets past the damper into the fireplace. Gray outside, the smell of ashes indoors. And my second narrow escape today came as I walked by the river, a river smaller than the one of my youth, but big enough. I was walking the dog, and the river tempted me terribly, flowing by so close. I'd sink like a lump of lead, and never think about any of this again. (Never again be old, living alone, either.) But there was Riley, old Riley, slouching along ahead of me, his old doggy, black and tan hips shaking. What would I do, let go the leash and leave him on his own? I'd never do that. He counts on me, he's expecting me to be here dishing up his supper and patting his head from here on out.

You're depressed, my daughter says, go to the doctor. I tell her I don't want to get started on pills. Will a pill tell me I wasn't a fool back then? I wouldn't take its word for anything. Soon there'll be a sunny morning when I can put it aside, when I can see how long ago it was and how little it should have mattered in the end. I have been through this before now, and it's passed.

There are the memories from earlier times, of course; they are what I should think of. The August night of a Perseid shower when we lay on quilts spread on the grass in her backyard and watched the stars fall. They fell almost continuously: "Look, look, there's another!" For us back then the stars were not masses of ionized gas whirling in fiery turbulence, but beautiful fixed points that once in a while lost their moorings in the heavens and streaked down the sky.

Our fathers stand by the pump house, talking, their heads cocked toward the sky. Our mothers move around inside the lighted house, talking as they tidy up the kitchen. Soon they will come out and lie down on a quilt too. The cats, who live outdoors, will walk around and over us, purring. The stars will go on falling all night, and we will sleep there together, at peace, our lives, fresh and barely used, still before us.

The Stash

Ɑ℈

A WOMAN RUSHED UP TO Glenna in the parking lot of the supermarket that morning—a pale woman with a blotchy complexion and a mass of pulled-back dark hair. "I thought you were my mother! She passed away last month—for a minute there you looked just like her!" The woman seemed agitated yet somehow proud, as if Glenna would find this news interesting and even complimentary.

Glenna pulled the strap of her bag higher on her shoulder. The woman wasn't that much younger than she was herself; how could she possibly be taken for her mother?

"I'm sorry," she said. She touched the woman's shoulder lightly. "Well—have a good day."

Had she really said "Have a good day"? In the store, studying the offerings at the fish counter, she thought of the encounter with annoyance. I could have told her about *my* mother, she thought, with a kind of lofty bitterness.

And what would her mother have done in her place? She'd have put her arm around the woman and said, "She's better off than we are, hon," which was the kind of thing she said to the bereaved at funerals. Kindhearted to a fault, that was her mother. Once in this same Miami neighborhood—not a very good neighborhood, though this was a good store—a raffish-looking young woman had been standing out on the sidewalk at eight o'clock in the morning calling, "Help me! Won't somebody please help me!" standing there holding a cucumber, and Glenna's mother, out shopping early, stopped the car and said, "Get in. Where you need to go?" and had driven the woman to the projects.

"That was dumb, Mama," Glenna said. "*Anything* could have happened to you, anything!"

"Pooh. I can tell about people," her mother said contemptuously. "Did anything happen? No. That poor girl—she was upset. She said, 'My uncle'll kill me if he finds out I was gone all night.' Holding that cucumber! But I just hate it the way people won't get *involved*."

Her mother wasn't driving any more. Glenna took her mother's car out every few weeks—on a fair day, because the roof leaked. "You don't need to keep the battery up—might as well sell it," her mother said dispiritedly—as if the bother would be worth the two hundred or so the car would bring. Her mother's cancer was in remission, but she was not strong. "I'll never drive any more." "Sure you will," Glenna said. She wasn't sure why she was keeping the battery up; it had simply become a habit. Driving the car made her irritable; she would start thinking of the sickness. For a while it hurt like having three babies at one time, her mother said. She would start thinking of her brother Clayton, who wanted her to look for her mother's stash of pills, the pills she'd hoarded against the future. Thinking of Clayton and the pills and the pain, she would soon be speeding, trying to outrun it all, and the little car would quiver beneath her.

Clayton had fallen out of a plane, and not long after that had been born again.

No one knew how far he'd fallen. Twelve or fifteen feet, he said, but Glenna thought he might have tumbled out just after it hit the ground. It was a light plane, piloted by a seventy-one-year-old pilot, one of his mysterious friends, who'd also been banged up in the crash. Clayton had broken some ribs and had a scar slanting above his upper lip; it gave him a supercilious, curled-lip expression. "When they checked you over in the hospital, I hope they checked your brains too," his mother said tartly. "Going up with that old man, oh Lord." She loved Clayton beyond measure.

In the Navy, Clayton had been trained as an electrician. When he got out after twenty years, he and a partner opened a repair shop. He and his wife had divorced years ago, and Glenna had expected to see him often. She loved him and forgave him for being the favored child; she imagined him sitting at the dining room table after dinner, talking, the way it had been when he'd come home on leave. He had the wide-ranging, quirky knowledge of the self-educated, and talked with great authority about whatever he was reading at the moment; he could tell you about the different kinds of sharks, about Benjamin Franklin's private life, about early Miami history. (The Seminoles' alligator wrestling was not traditional, but something an entertainment promoter had taught them.) He was six years older than she was, and he'd always explained things to her—that the cat was going to have kittens, look at her stomach; that there was no sound if a tree fell in the forest and no one was there. He was smart, he was good looking; he seemed a kind of validation of her family. Her parents, who had run a chronically failing wholesale grocery business, had been smart, but you might not have guessed it to look at them.

But Clayton didn't visit as often as she'd hoped. She wondered if he spent his evenings in bars, and had an occasional one-night stand.

After the plane crash, he was a long time recovering. He denied, though, that it had had anything to do with his joining the evangelical church. "I felt the need to do it, that's all. My life changed, and I'm thankful."

He visited their mother more often after he joined the church. He had a church girlfriend now, and brought her occasionally—a tall, quiet young woman with long light hair, who had kissed his mother, taking her somewhat aback. He'd come alone the Sunday afternoon that his mother had told him about the pills. That was at Glenna's, where her mother lived now, in the guest suite down the hall from the other bedrooms. Glenna hadn't been present when her mother confided in Clayton. "I'm not going to hurt that much anymore. I'll just end it, that's all," her mother told him. "I saved out some pills, and I'll take 'em and ask God to forgive me, and go on to sleep."

"No, no, you mustn't do that, Mama," Clayton had told her. "We'll make sure they give you enough medication. Don't do it. It would be wrong."

Over the phone he said to Glenna, "You need to find 'em. Don't flush 'em down the toilet, though. Stuff gets in the groundwater—they say there's Prozac in it now—think it'll make us all get along better?"—jollying her along to muffle the urgency of his tone. "Wrap 'em in some newspaper and put 'em in the garbage.

You don't need to tell her—she'll just think she misplaced 'em. We can't let her do it. It would be wrong." She gave him credit for not saying straight out, "a sin."

"Hmm. I'm supposed to go rummaging through her things? How long has she had them, I wonder—they may be expired by now anyway."

"Look for 'em, look for 'em."

She looked through her mother's bathroom medicine cabinet, feeling annoyed. She mentioned it to her husband, Hugh. He was an ophthalmologist, and when he got home at night he wanted amusement; now, instead of the dog races or jai-alai, it was television or cards. Sometimes, after an afternoon of surgery, his hands shook a little as they played.

"Mama worries about the pain she might have if she has a recurrence," she said as they played gin rummy.

He took a while to answer, studying the cards in his hand. "Pain management is improving. She'll have to complain, though. Tell her that."

"Oh, she didn't say anything to me about it. She told Clayton."

She went on thinking about it. She was thinking about it the next afternoon when her daughter Mara came in from out front, where she had been talking to a neighbor boy, lying on her back in the seat of her car, bare feet out the window, smoking. "I thought you were quitting," Glenna said.

"I am, I am. That was the first one I'd had all day. I know, I know. I won't smoke in the house, I promise you. I'm going to quit. Really."

"Your father's in the health business, in case you've forgotten. And here's your grandma, trying to be well and keep going . . . She worries about having a recurrence. The pain. She may be hoarding some pills. To end it all if it gets too bad." Commit suicide, kill herself?—she didn't like any way there was of saying it.

"Oh, no!" Mara cried. "They wouldn't let her be in pain at the hospital, would they?" Her well-made-up eyes were full of alarm. Why was it so persuasive, that lovely, big-eyed, touchingly sincere ignorance? "You want me to talk to her and tell her not to worry?"

"No. She doesn't know I know." Odd that her mother had told Clayton and not herself. Well, not so odd; it made him the favored one again.

"Daddy knows people at the hospital, he has some clout. He could see that they take good care of her, couldn't he?"

Her mother had moved in six months before. Earlier, when she was weakened from chemotherapy, Glenna had said to Hugh, "I think my mother had better move in with us." He'd raised his eyebrows and said, "If you think so." He didn't dislike her mother; he patted her shoulder and didn't pay much attention to her. Once in a while something she said amused him and he would repeat it to friends. "She says, when she has to redo something, 'I'll have to lick my calf over again.' Those old rural sayings are wonderful. I hope they don't die out." Even that got on Glenna's nerves. Was his own family so highfalutin? They were perfectly ordinary, decent people, hardworking and Methodist, like her mother; a little more prosperous, a little more citified, that was all.

"If you think so" had not pleased Glenna. Instead of moving her mother in, she'd begun to spend nights in her mother's apartment off and on, sometimes two or three in a row, going back to her house during the day. It was a message to Hugh. In a couple of weeks he said, "Sure, move your mother in. There's plenty of room."

Her mother considered the accommodations quite luxurious. She liked the pool, though she never went in. Sometimes she went out and sat beside it, doing nothing, contemplating the green water. What was she thinking about? Red Bug Pond, back in Georgia, where they used to live? "Oh, nothing, just dreaming along," she said.

This afternoon she was going to take her mother for a drive. "Anywhere in particular you want to go?" she'd asked at breakfast.

Her mother was sloshing coffee around in her mouth like mouthwash, possibly removing something from her dental plate. "Well. I've got the address of that place—I wouldn't mind going by there some time." There was a murder trial going on, and her mother had written down the address where the crime had taken place. "I guess I'm a curiosity-seeker. I don't care, I just like to see where it happened." In the days when she was still driving, she sometimes got lost searching for some such address, and would ask a passerby for directions, preferably some downtrodden-looking person who often knew neither the neighborhood nor much English. Once she and a friend had been so preoccupied with the search that she ran a stop sign and got a ticket.

"Want to take your car?" Glenna asked. "It may need the exercise." Hugh had taken the Rabbit that morning, leaving the silver-green Mercedes, more likely to attract attention if they parked near a house in an iffy neighborhood.

"No, let's take yours," her mother said contentedly. She loved the Mercedes, and watched for others on the streets.

The crime scenes she'd driven her mother past were painfully ordinary, usually a common Miami house, pastel stucco with a graying white tile roof and a chain link fence, set back the same distance from the street as its neighbors. (How could a house remain so outwardly commonplace with such uncommon feelings festering inside?) Today's house was in the old northwest part of town, not far from where they'd lived when Glenna was growing up. An old street; an old house set at the extreme back of a lot, beyond wildly overgrown foliage.

"This yard's a jungle," her mother murmured as they turned into the rough, gouged track of a driveway. They got out; her mother toiled up the drive beside her, stalking along in her shoes, pulling her legs up out of them like a child playing dress-up. Age had given her a guinea-hen shape, then illness had left her small and curveless.

It was a small white frame house, low to the ground; it made her think of playhouses, of Hansel and Gretel in the forest. It was a gift to her mother, this secluded, out-of-the-way scene that imagination could easily make sinister. It would thrill her. There was no police tape; the crime had taken place nearly a year before.

There was a screened porch in front, behind red and yellow speckled croton bushes. On the porch, a forgotten, dried-up houseplant on a shelf, and two chairs stacked together upside down. Another bit of porch in back, sagging forward, holding worn-down brooms, a stack of yellowed newspapers, and a jumble of things in a washtub.

"It was a fellow she'd befriended," her mother said. "I think he did some work for her, and they got friendly. He moved in, and then he killed her. They say they were lovers—looks to me like she was pretty old for that. Living here by herself, oh Lord. I think about people that get murdered—they don't know if anybody'll ever know what happened, if they'll ever be *avenged*."

"I doubt they think about it, they're too busy trying not to get murdered."

"People ought to die thinking everything's in order, everything'll be all right. Peaceful."

And without too much pain. She might as well admit it: she was hurt her mother hadn't told her, only Clayton.

Her mother walked on around the porch, peering in. There were voices from the house behind them, beyond a ragged hedge. An adolescent girl's face appeared for an instant, peering at them through parted greenery, then disappeared.

"Maybe we should go before we upset the neighbors."

"Sure . . . You think this is tacky, don't you?" The insult of illness had made her mother feisty, and she answered it back at random.

"Sure, it's tacky." Tacky as the true crime magazines her mother read. "I drove you over, didn't I? It's okay with me."

"That poor woman, that poor woman." Her mother's face crumpled; she began to cry.

"Well, she's beyond pain now. Don't cry!" She took her mother's arm when she stumbled on a rut in the driveway. "Maybe she's at peace now that he's on trial." She ignored the falsity of that, and the sad falsity of her mother's shifting her sorrow to this unknown woman. Her mother's crying had always unnerved her. As a small child, she'd cried whenever her mother cried; she had sobbed at the funerals of people she'd never met. At home, in the kitchen, her mother had sung the songs of her own childhood, about orphans and starving Irish children, and throughout her childhood her chief anxiety had been that her mother might die.

Her childhood churchgoing had been left behind some time during nursing school and shift work in the hospital. Then Mara had come home from school in the second grade and asked, "What are we? Everybody's *something*—are we Catholic or Baptist or what?" Hugh voted for the Unitarian Church, and they had gone there. The Unitarians hadn't talked much about sin, though. Now, driving through these familiar but degraded streets, the streets of the past, she felt a momentary yearning for the church-going days of childhood, everything clear-cut and simple. Back then, she'd known what to believe about everything.

Her mother had dried her eyes. "It's sure changed along here. Guns and bail bonds! Checks cashed. Army surplus. Oh Lord."

When her father died, Glenna had been on her first job. She'd been sad, she'd missed him, but she was young and busy, and newly in love with Hugh. She was closer to her mother. And yet she had hesitated to move her mother into her house—why pretend the hesitation had all been Hugh's? She didn't like the extravagant praise her mother gave the next-door neighbor at her tiny apartment in south Dade. "She makes those children mind too. She doesn't put up with any nonsense."

"The way we do?" Glenna said, and her mother made a dismissive noise, not quite a denial. Her mother got on her nerves, listening closely to what they said over the phone to Hughie, off at college, eager to take part in any family drama and give advice. Mara's bare feet and tattoos disturbed her whenever she noticed them. "Here it's taken all these years to get us Southerners in shoes, and now you kids go barefooted!" "Sure, it's a pretty little butterfly, but you'll get tired of it, and it won't ever wear off, will it." Mara, seventeen and supremely confident, would laugh and pat her grandmother's arm.

It was late afternoon; the traffic was thickening. It surged and halted and surged again. Gleaming white clouds were piled high in the sky; now, in October, the heat was abating. Under the muscular, intertwined banyans of Coral Way, a few leaves had fallen on the center parkway.

"Do you ever miss fall, real fall?" she asked.

"Maybe a little bit. It was nice in the fall, back in Georgia. But your dad couldn't get much work up there. Maybe I missed the spring more. The lilacs."

Small towns in Georgia: they'd lived there when she was very young. "I've got a dim memory of an old house with a fireplace in most of the rooms."

"Yes. I broiled meat over the coals for Brother"—that was Clayton—"he wanted it like the Indians ate, he said. And I read aloud to us after supper most nights—you'd be sitting in Daddy's lap. We had some good times! But your dad couldn't get much going up there, so we came down here. More opportunities."

All those years, all the memories stored in her mother's head and only there. She tried to think of a question to ask about the old days.

The traffic halted at a red light. The driver in the next car stared at their car with what seemed to be casual hostility.

At home, Mara's car was in the garage; there was a sound of music far away in the house. Getting out of the car, with Glenna's help, her mother sighed, straightening up. A kind of shudder ran through her, as though a transitory pain had come and gone, and she gave a little head shake, as if saying no to whatever she felt. "I guess I'll go lie down a while," she said.

Over the phone, Clayton said, speaking softly, "D'you find the pills?"

"I checked the medicine chest. Nothing there."

"Look around. Look in her nightstand and her bureau drawers. Please look."

"Oh, Clayton. Well, all right."

She'd look some time. That week she was gathering up things for a benefit sale, and went into her mother's room. "Anything you want to get rid of?" She fought off the thought that one of these days the whole kit and caboodle would go. She slid her mother's closet door open and glanced at the shelf. "How about that white summer handbag—you never liked it."

Her mother looked alarmed. "No, no." She was struggling for words and struggling to get up from the chaise. "No, I need it, leave it alone! There's some belts there on a hook, they're too big for me now, you can have them."

The white handbag: that must be where the pills were. Glenna believed in them for the first time. She plucked the belts off the hook and said, "Thanks."

Clayton was there on Sunday, without his girlfriend. Ordinarily the two of them would talk to Glenna and Hugh for a while, then go up to her mother's room. Sometimes her mother came down instead, moving cautiously down the steps, and when Clayton or his girl asked how she was, she'd say, "*Old*, that's how I am. Old. There's no cure for it." Mostly she listened silently as the others talked.

This afternoon Clayton murmured as soon as he came in, "D'you find 'em?"

Glenna shook her head warningly, gesturing upward, and murmured, "She's got new hearing aids, remember." It was an excuse not to talk. Clayton went upstairs, and she sat down again to the Sunday paper spread out around her on the long sofa.

But she didn't read; she stared out through the glass doors to the patio, thinking what to say to Clayton when he came back down. It seemed to her his visit with her mother was going on longer than usual.

He came stepping lightly down the stairs. "She seems to be feeling pretty fair today," he said, and came over to stand in front of her.

"I know what you're going to say, but don't say it! I'm not going to search for those pills." It flashed across her mind to say that they were in the white handbag, and what was he going to do about it? "Just don't ask me to any more." It sounded harsher than she'd expected.

"Oh. Well—" He sat down beside her, looking at her solicitously, as if she'd stubbed her toe. "You're mad. Don't be mad." His look was kindly, as if he meant to counsel her. "There's no need to get upset." The scar above his upper lip made him look slightly scornful; she still wasn't quite used to it.

"Is this some religious thing?"

"Oh—well, I just think we can't let her take 'em. Listen, wouldn't you feel terrible if she took 'em? Do you want her to die?"

"What a silly question. You're in denial, Clayton." It wasn't what she'd planned to say. "Those pills are her business, that's all. That's all I'm saying. Just don't keep asking me to look for them."

He raised his eyebrows and did a massive shrug, as if shrinking before her. She'd spoken more sharply than she'd ever spoken to him before. They sat in silence, waiting for some peace to descend.

"Well. Okay, then," he said suddenly, and got up. "Sorry I've upset you."

"I'm not upset. I just wanted to make it clear."

"You have. Okay. See you later." And he was gone.

Not a big disagreement, really, and yet more of one than they'd ever had before. They'd get over it, of course; it would be all right in a week or so. It irked her that, all the same, she felt a little uneasiness.

She closed her eyes in a moment of wordless prayer, then turned to the refuge of the Sunday paper.

Upstairs, their mother had gone out to the landing, thinking to call a question down to Clayton before he left, though as she heard them talking she forgot what the question had been. They were fussing about something—the pills, and her dying. She was sorry for them. The pain of her own mother's death—she didn't like to remember it even now. Glenna seemed more resigned than Clayton, maybe a little too resigned. He couldn't bear to see her go, he'd always needed her, and starting off to school as a small boy he'd called out desperately, "Bye, Mama, bye, Mama!" It had been a mistake to tell him about the pills, but the most urgent thoughts had a way of popping out to someone close to you.

If she ever took the pills she'd write a note and say she was sorry, they must understand, she'd done her best not to do this. Probably the pills would remain, wrapped in several tissues, inside a small zippered compartment within the white summer handbag on the closet shelf. She didn't think of them often, only once in a while when a random pain came, maybe one that had nothing to do with the cancer. She moved within a dream now, and the images that came within her dreams at night were as real as the days'—her father on his customary bench in the country church, beside an open window held up by a stick; the moss at the bottom of the tub where the farm mules drank.

Once in a while, when some thought jerked her up short and made her suddenly look at death head-on, she reminded herself of the bad ways there were to go—in a fire, drowning, murdered like the poor woman whose house she'd looked at. She would die in her bed, or a comfortable hospital bed with people trying to help her, offering tender care, be grateful. She moved through the days, holding off thought.

She would have to help Clayton and Glenna get past this little disagreement. No, it might be better not to speak of it. She could think about it later. Now she was tired from the visit and she went back to her room and stretched out on the bed, pulled the folded-up throw over her feet, and closed her eyes. In a few minutes she would be somewhere else, perhaps back in Georgia in the house of many fireplaces, the children playing outside, herself young and well, the way she was meant to be.

Or I Shall Not Get Home Tonight

༼ঌ

THE FIRST THING THAT DAY was losing my watch. Or, rather, not losing it.

It was the third day of our trip, and Ralph and I had eaten breakfast in the motel restaurant. It was when we went back up to the room that I noticed I didn't have the watch on. I looked on the bedside table, under the bed, and around the room. No watch, so I took the elevator back down and went to the booth where we'd been sitting. There were some other people in it, of course; I told them the trouble and they got up and looked around the seats and under the table, quite concerned, so nice. No watch. I apologized and thanked them several times and took the elevator back up. I looked around the room again, gave up, and started packing. It was when I reached up to pull something off one of the fixed hangers that I saw the watch; it was on my wrist the whole time. Well, I thought, that's just how things are going. Did any of those people in the booth see it poking out from under my sleeve and think: we are dealing with a crazy woman here?

Ralph had stretched out on one of the beds when I'd gone back downstairs, and now he was asleep, so I lay down too and drifted off. It had been a rough night. He hadn't wanted me to lock the door, then he'd be trapped inside; everywhere he was, he worried about a way out. Upstairs in our house he asked if there was an outside door up there, and I explained we didn't want one, we'd step out into nothing and break our necks. When I insisted on locking the motel room door, he began to phone everyone he knew in this town to come spring him. Luckily most of them hadn't answered. They'd gone to bed away from the phone, or if they answered once, they wouldn't have again, so nobody came pounding on the door to get him out. I got a little ragged sleep, between his phone calls. Maybe he slept a little, I don't know.

This after-breakfast nap was glorious sleep for about half an hour, then I woke up as the door closed behind him. It woke me up fast, and I grabbed my purse and the room key and smoothed my hair and started off, but the elevator was slow coming, and some other people stopped it on other floors, and when I got down to the lobby he was nowhere in sight. I asked at the desk if they'd seen him go out, and they said he'd turned toward town.

What if he fell crossing the street, say?—he fell every few months. We were in a pretty Florida college town, but it was not known for being crime-free. He was frail, and he was careless about showing his money; I imagined him mugged, lying some-where in an alley next to garbage cans. I went back inside and asked the people at the desk to call the police for me. Perhaps not wise, but we didn't have much "wise" at our house those days.

The cop who came out was truculent; this wasn't his idea of police work. He frowned and kept on frowning. He said he'd drive me around to look, and he let his wrath out on a bum sleeping under a hedge at the back of the motel parking lot. I nearly jumped when he yelled, "You better not be here when I get back or I'm lockin' you up!"

I figured he was blaming me for letting Ralph out of my sight, so I explained that he was all right part of the time, that's the way it was with this disease; he'd be different in the afternoon from how he was in the morning, and vice versa. We drove around and around and I said that was enough looking, he couldn't have walked any farther than that, and he took me back to the motel. "The next step is an APB," he said. I said we ought to give it a little time, he might show up back here, and the cop went away, still frowning, probably to check the hedge for the bum, hoping to throw him in jail.

And so I set off up the street; I was going to go over the neighborhood with a fine-tooth comb. It was a street of little shops, heading away from the campus toward town, and I peered into the shops as I passed, unlikely as they looked—a jewelry store, an optometrist's, a coin and stamp shop. A sweaty young man in silky-looking shorts and a band around his hair came running by and I called, "Hey, listen, if you see an old man looking kind of lost, wave or something, okay?" and he turned, running in place, and nodded. "You got it," and he jogged on off.

A middle-aged woman coming out of an Indian gift shop heard me, and she stopped and stared at me, so I said, "I'm looking for my husband—he's disappeared."

"Just now?"

No, last week, you ninny. "He walked off from the Holiday Inn down there." She was staring at me as if I were the one *lacking*, so I had to tell her everything. I wasn't particularly drawn to her,

her splashy outfit and fussy bangs, not that she was necessarily drawn to me either; I hadn't had time to comb my hair or look in the mirror. But I liked the way she nodded sympathetically.

A young guy, big and kind of shapeless, all baby fat, trotted up, and she said, "Ralph is here, he'll find him! My son, Ralph. She's looking for *her* Ralph—describe him."

I couldn't remember what Ralph was wearing to save my life. He didn't like short-sleeved shirts, though, he said they had no style, so I said, "He's an older guy, gray-haired, long-sleeved shirt, his head's kind of sunk down on his shoulders . . ."

"Ralph will find him," his mother said, and Ralph trotted off in his gleaming white running shoes.

A pretty young woman, probably a student, was passing us on the sidewalk, and Ralph's mother said to her, "If you see an elderly gentleman up ahead that looks kind of lost, give us a sign, wave or something. He's lost."

"Oh, sure," the girl said, and hurried along a little faster. I had a vision of a whole line of people looking for Ralph, as in a fairy tale, one of them named something like Foolish Hans, holding a goose under his arm. He'd be the one to find him.

But up ahead, young Ralph yelled, "Is this him?" loud enough to carry all the way back to the motel. He was in front of a laundromat, and when I got there and looked in, there was my Ralph, standing just inside the door, talking to some old woman.

"Yes," I said. "Yes! Thank you so much!" Ralph's mother wanted to hang around and hear what I was going to say, but young Ralph said, "Come on, Mom."

"We've got to go, honey," I said. My Ralph stared at me, looking surly. He said nothing. The woman he'd been talking to, a small, dark woman with skin the Florida sun had had its way with, stared at both of us, listening, but in a friendly way. She wasn't as old as I'd first thought, just heavily tanned and wrinkled. "We've got a plane to catch. We've got to go home."

"I'm not going," Ralph said. "I'm not going anywhere with you. You're part of the enemy."

"You want to spend another night in the Holiday Inn? You were miserable there last night! That's where we'll be if we miss that plane, you know. We've got to go home."

"Where's home?" the woman standing by asked in an easygoing kind of way.

I didn't see that it was any of her business, but Ralph said, "Illinois. Downstate," surprising me.

"Come on, honey, we've got to go."

"I'm not going."

"Oh, you know you want to go home," the woman said. "Sure you do."

I went back out to the sidewalk. It was one of those moments when, after all these years, I want a cigarette again—as if one wouldn't make me deathly sick. If there'd been a store right there, I might have bought a pack, though. I didn't mind his being annoyed with me, that was routine, but we had a problem here.

The other Ralph and his mother were standing by a car, talking. "He won't budge," I said. They looked concerned.

The woman from the laundromat was coming down the sidewalk toward me. "Look, honey, I think I might get him moving, I've had experience with this kind of a situation. I remind him of somebody he used to know. What room are you in?" I told her, and she said, "I'll try to get him down there."

I can't believe I relied on her—but it seemed reasonable at the moment. I walked on back, the morning sun getting warmer, the steady traffic passing on the street and stopping for the traffic light just ahead, down by the motel, or turning into the service station on the corner across the street. The woman reminded me of somebody, too, an old friend from high school, a girl with merry eyes and a cynical mouth, and in my mind I was calling her Kat.

And I was thinking of a fairy tale. I couldn't quite remember it, which was disappointing, considering the years I put in as a children's librarian. It's the one where the old woman is trying to get home and some creature, I think a pig, won't jump over the stile, and a whole string of events must take place to get things moving: water, quench fire; fire, burn stick; stick, beat dog; dog, bite pig; pig, jump over stile—or I shall not get home tonight! I made up my own short sequence: Ralph, find Ralph; Kat, walk Ralph to motel—or I shall not get home tonight!

I went up in the elevator, and waited in our room. Pretty soon I heard voices, and I went to the door. Kat was walking him down the hall, her arm through his. "Here you are! You have a real good trip, now, Ralph, hear?" She withdrew her arm, kissed him goodbye, and moved away briskly. Presently Ralph shambled in.

I was already packing his bag. "Hi, honey. I've arranged with the motel van, they'll pick us up in an hour. Get the extra soaps in the bathroom and the lotion, will you—they just throw them out. Let's go down to the restaurant and order some sandwiches to take along, you know they don't give you anything much on the plane any more."

I did not let it occur to me that he might turn around at the door of the plane and refuse to go in, or that he might want to get out after we reached twenty thousand feet. No, I'll tell you the truth, it did occur to me, but I worked hard to hold it off. I took the window seat in case it would make him feel hemmed in. We raced along the runway, and I fastened my attention on the landscape below, treetops and then a lake, as we rose through shreds of cloud, up and up to where the clouds lay below us like a grayed snowfield thick enough to walk out on. Then I saw he was already asleep.

I was sorry I hadn't been able to explain to everyone why we'd tried to travel, considering the shape he was in. He was the one who took the call about his brother's dying. If I'd taken it, I'd have said, I'm so sorry, so terribly sorry, and I wish we could come for the service, but you know Ralph's condition, and my sister-in-law would surely have said, Of course, don't even think about it. But he took the call and he was keen to go; he started packing right away, and later he got up in the middle of the night to revise his packing. I think he believed that if he left home he would leave the sickness behind; in a new place everything would be different. He'd have been heartbroken if I'd said we couldn't go. The first flight was all right, even the first night in the motel was all right, maybe because he was so tired.

But when we got dressed the next morning to go to the service, he'd suddenly looked at me in dismay and said, "I can't give a talk this morning." He was thinking we were at one of the conferences he used to attend. "That's okay, you're not scheduled to speak today," I said.

In the church, after the main part of the service, when people were getting up and giving their recollections and so on, he turned to me and murmured, "Who are they talking about?" and I told him it was his brother Paul. He raised his eyebrows, surprised. At the house he managed well enough, talking to the few old relatives and the young nieces and nephews; they seemed to pull him into the normal. One of them drove us back to the motel afterward, talking all the way, Ralph mostly quiet; he seemed to be thinking.

Is return a relief or a regret? I used to ask myself that as the plane began to descend at the end of a vacation. Back to the same old stuff—but the strains of travel are over. Usually for me it's a toss-up, but this time more of a relief.

He woke up shortly before we landed, and asked suddenly, "Who wrote *When We Dead Awaken,* was it Strindberg or Ibsen?"

"I've forgotten," I said. "We'll have to look it up." We had come to a normal patch.

It was after dark. Below the window there were the patterns of tiny yellow lights down below, mysterious in the wide and lonely darkness.

The van driver met us near baggage claim, as arranged, holding up a sign with our name on it. It was a thick-waisted, middle-aged woman. In the van she was very talkative as we hurtled along the highway in the dark. She confided that she was pregnant, pregnant with twins. She'd been married before and had some kids, but had a different husband now, and he wanted some children. He was out in the field on the tractor, working right now, after dark, because it had been too wet to work for a while.

"That's a shame," Ralph said. "Well, maybe the good weather will hold. Congratulations on your twins."

Then we were at our house, our cream-colored Georgian with the dignified broken pediment over the front door—our house with no exit on the second floor. He's asked me several times how long we've lived here, and is always surprised when I say thirty-one years. Why is it then so unfamiliar, so easy to get lost in?

We unlocked the front door by the light of the van's headlights, and waved goodbye.

"Wasn't that interesting," Ralph said. "Hubby out in the field, working after dark. And she pregnant with twins, like it's all in a day's work. That's youth, I guess."

"She wasn't all that young."

He turned and gave me a sweet and significant smile, then a gentle embrace, there with our bags at our feet. What was he remembering? His smile said we had a little life left.

I could say that I remembered the early years, necking in the music-listening rooms in college, and that first married summer when it was almost too hot for two bodies to come together; the companionship of all those years, agreement on so much, one of us saying excitedly to the other, "Have you read *this*?" or "That's exactly right!" But of course I felt only the vague, customary sense of all that. Those other years—they're something in the blood or deep in the cells, something long assimilated, supplying the strength for whatever happens later. Not quite enough, but almost. I must have known then that things wouldn't get better, they could only grow worse. But that evening, at that peaceful moment, I gave my poor stooped darling a warm hug, thinking with amazement: somehow I got home tonight.